BESTSELLER

Ahmed Faiyaz is the bestselling author of *Love, Life & All That Jazz…*, *Another Chance*, *Scammed* and the editor of the *Urban Shots*. He was born and raised in Bengaluru. Apart from being a passionate writer, he dabbles with film-making and travels to lesser-known destinations to better understand life and the times we live in.

He lives and works in Dubai, with his two boys and their tabby cat named, Bob.

BESTSELLER

Ahmed Faiyaz

RUPA

Published by
Rupa Publications India Pvt. Ltd 2018
7/16, Ansari Road, Daryaganj
New Delhi 110002

Sales Centres:
Allahabad Bengaluru Chennai
Hyderabad Jaipur Kathmandu
Kolkata Mumbai

ISBN: 978-93-5333-264-8

First impression 2018

10 9 8 7 6 5 4 3 2 1

The moral right of the author has been asserted.

Dedicated to Zahir & Kabir

Day 1

'So, what do you do, sir?' the affable taxi driver asked in chaste Hindi while he navigated his beaten-up taxi through potholes and mind-boggling traffic. He wiped his brow with a large handkerchief and squinted, straining to see the vehicles ahead.

'I am a writer,' I said in a low voice. *Of a book that's gathering cobwebs! I'm also an editor who was recently fired.*

'*Acha*, you're here to write for films,' the taxi driver concluded.

'Er...I'm not sure. I wrote a book that was published last year. I'm not sure what I'll write next.'

'I *was* in the film industry once. So many years as an assistant to filmmakers! I worked with Dev Anand, Shammi Kapoor, Rajesh Khanna...' He turned up the volume of the old Hindi song that blared from his squeaky cassette player.

'That's impressive!'

'I went on to make my own film as a producer and director— *Nanhe Rahi,* starring Rajiv Kumar and Heena Masood. You know she became the #1 actress; everyone was in love with her.'

'So how come you're driving a cab now?' I asked him inquisitively.

'Arey sahib, that's my fate. The film took six years to make;

Rajiv Kumar left his wife and ran off with some hippie for eight months. During this period, Heena Masood got married and resumed shooting only after she had had her first child; it was a horrible phase and the film flopped badly. I lost a lot of money—even my apartment had to be sold off to pay for the debts—and with all that stress and pressure I started drinking a lot. From being a producer, I couldn't go back to being an assistant director, na? So, after my wife left me and went back to her village, I began driving this taxi to fill my stomach. I have a big family back in Kanpur…'

'What did you say your name was?'

He turned around and grinned, showing his broken teeth. 'Pyarelal, sahib! In the film industry, I was known as Master Pyare. In those days…'

'Why is it so hot?' I interrupted.

He turned around abruptly, looking baffled. 'Arey, this is winter, sahib. The heat begins in March. Where are you from?'

'London…'

'*Acha*, I had hoped to make a film there…but life, you know, sahib,' he said softly, as he swerved dangerously into one of the bylanes and the song hit a high note. A few metres ahead, I got off and tipped him generously.

Sweating profusely, I entered the decrepit building with much trepidation. This certainly was a far cry from the swanky publishing office in Covent Garden I was used to. The building complex seemed more like a ghetto that housed sweatshops. I walked past tailors, artisans of all kinds, a makeshift flour mill, a guy frying pakoras and jalebis in a hole in the wall, and other sweaty bodies that moved around with a sense of purpose. For a moment, I thought I had ended up in the wrong place.

'Ram Lal Mills, Parel'—the rusted board read. It was a poorly lit and unkempt staircase, littered with paper cups and empty wrappers of chips and chocolates. I dragged my feet up the stairs, wondering why one of India's oldest publishers was located in this heap of garbage. I walked through the corridor and soon came across a dusty wooden door that had a little wooden sign—Kalim Publishing, Since 1951. This certainly wasn't what I had imagined it to be. I had expected it to be a nice and cozy office on Marine Drive, overlooking the Arabian Sea. But I was in Mumbai—and this was it.

I entered to see a slender, dusky woman doing her nails, and an old man sitting at a desk not far from her, reading a newspaper.

'Excuse me,' I said with as much enthusiasm as I could muster. *Fucking hell! Is this the only job I can get? Damn this recession!*

She looked up and seemed irritated. There was a magazine, a purse, a phone extension and a little potted cactus on her desk. There was no sign of a computer or a laptop.

'What do you want?' she said with a look of annoyance.

'Er...we spoke on the phone. You must be Sita. I'm Akshay Mathur...I just got in from London. I'm here for a meeting with Mr Kalim.'

'Ah yes! Come in sir, sorry. A lot of salesmen come here, you know, to sell credit cards, home loans, personal loans...'

'Er...sure. I can imagine.'

'Why don't you wait there?' she said, pointing in the direction of a ragged sofa at the other end of the room, next to a wooden cupboard. 'Mr Kalim usually comes in at 11 a.m. He stays nearby.'

'Okay, I had set up a time of 9 o' clock, if I'm right. Perhaps he can see me rightaway?'

'Yes, please sit down. He'll be here shortly,' she said with a grimace. The old man with the newspaper continued poring over it without looking up even once.

With some hesitation, I sat there and looked around the barren office, finding little interest in the outdated Bollywood film glossies that lay on a little table in front of me. What choice did I have? I was 34, divorced, a failed writer and a former editor of the now-defunct *Metro* magazine, which published its last issue two months ago. The stupid decisions I had made over the years run rampant in my mind—taking a job driven by my idealism to work for an iconic but floundering magazine at a time when print media was dying, falling in love with my former flatmate, Janice, marrying fucking Janice, drinking too much, gathering way too much debt, thanks to the EMIs for that flashy Mini Cooper, despite riding on the Tube to work every day, working for a boorish real estate shark who had taken over *Metro* and knew nothing about publishing or had any sensibility to publish a magazine on art and culture, and, of course, writing that self-indulgent book that most critics tore apart, despite the fact that it got shortlisted for the Commonwealth Writers' Prize. What the fuck was I thinking?

A while later, as I was beginning to doze off, Sita called out to me. 'Mr Mathur, you can go in now. Mr Kalim is waiting for you.'

I entered a little cabin with an old wooden desk and wooden chairs. Everything in the room looked like it had been preserved since the 1950s. There were pictures of Mr Kalim with prime ministers and other luminaries who had died decades ago. An old man, with a heavy frame, thickset glasses and a well-preserved waistcoat that had clearly seen better days, slouched over the table and looked at me with a contemptuous grin.

'Hmm... Mr Akshay Mathur. So, they sent you here to be our editor?' Angus Lee, a friend from Cambridge, had got me this job. His father had taken a majority stake in Kalim Publishing more than a year ago and had since then kept the firm afloat.

'I assume they have.' Thomson Lee's *Lee Pocket Books* was quite well known in the UK. Buying a majority stake in Kalim Publishing was their attempt to enter the promising Indian market.

'Yes, well, maybe if they interfere less on the editorial side of the business it will be good. As a condition of the terms we agreed to, I will stay on and remain head of editorial for two years.'

'Right... I believe we all understand that,' I said.

'So, they recruit you—some recently laid-off kid from an obscure British magazine—and they send you here to be the deputy editor of my company!' he screamed with his face turning red.

'I was asked to assist you in building a strong frontlist of titles. They want the business to grow.'

'What do *they* know about publishing, dammit? They print those silly books on zodiac signs and popular quotes,' the old buzzard said with some contempt, before he calmed down after a sip from his cup of tea. 'Anyway, settle down, it's your first day. Will you have a cup of coffee or cola?'

'Thanks! I'm alright.' I was a trifle thirsty, but I wanted to discuss what we had to and get out of that cabin as soon as possible.

'Hmm... So where do you want to begin?'

'Maybe you can tell me a little bit about the firm—the team, recent books and the list for the coming year.'

'Hmm…well, there's not so much to say. I take care of the editorial side of things. Mr Samuel, who is sitting outside, manages production, cover designs and sales, and Sita, my assistant, manages the office.'

'That's a very small set-up. How do…'

'We don't believe in wasting resources, Mr Aakash, or is it Akshay? We have been in the business over 70 years and are still here, aren't we? I came to this office when I was 21 and just out of college; it's been over 49 years since I took over from my father and I don't need people to teach me how to run my business,' he said, gritting his teeth. *Living in the past, are we?*

'I don't intend to, Mr Kalim. Could we discuss the recent titles and what we have coming up?' I spoke with as much restraint as possible. *Boy, this guy could have a stroke given how we're getting on.*

'Hmm…well! We did this book on the war in the 1960s. When was that? 2010, I think. Mr Samuel will give you the details—he maintains a register. It's in its second print run. We also published a book on the famous music director, R.V. Puri, written by his wife. It's also in its second print run now,' he said proudly.

'When was this?' I enquired.

'I think December 2009. We haven't done much in the last two years as I was mostly sick and went through a cardiac bypass surgery.' He sounded bitter, looking at me like I was some vermin who had crept into his office.

'I'm sorry,' I said in a concerned tone.

'We did a few reprints of children's books and some other

books from our backlist. We have a backlist of 140 books, you know. Over 25 are still in print.'

'That's interesting! What do we have planned for this year?'

'Planned titles for this year? Hmm...there is this book by the children's writer, Vinod Dutta: It's a collection of love stories, sort of.' He sat back and thought for a moment. 'Then, I'm pulling together this collection of stories called *Twilight*, from among writers I know. It's been lying with us for a while actually. There's also this collection of poems in Sanskrit that a friend, Romal Anand, is translating to Hindi and English. We should do something about that. It's going to be a busy year with three to four books.'

'Where do you get entries from? How do you evaluate manuscripts?'

'Sita!' he shouted. 'Get me another cup of masala chai,' he said, with some annoyance that was directed at me, as she opened the door and stuck her head in.

'You have a lot of questions ....' He sat back and regarded me patronizingly. 'Well, people post or drop off their manuscripts with Sita. We don't get too many of them these days. A few came in last year; I haven't looked at them. Maybe this is something that you could do.' He leaned back and scratched his chin, looking fatigued.

'Sure, but what about online presence? The website link says the address can't be found. Do we accept any entries via email? Do we have relationships with literary agents? Do we have a social media presence?'

'What? No, I don't know what all this is! I think we are happy using the methods we have in place. Sita keeps a register where she logs in new entries, and when we reject them; we send a postcard to the writer and let them know. If we like something, I write to the author stating our intention to publish the book. But I admit this hasn't happened in a while.' *I'm damn sure it hasn't, there are cobwebs here.*

'I see. Perhaps I should get started and begin reading manuscripts.'

'Perhaps you should. Although, I will have to take a close look at anything you recommend. We stand for something here, at Kalim.' *Sure, you stand for dusty old books and relics from the '70s.* 'I'm not a fan of the drivel that's written in the name of literature today. Some of these writers can't spell Wordsworth or Hemingway. Bloody buffoons!' he grunted before I crept out of his room and walked up to Sita, who had begun to regard me with hostility and as a pest. *Whew! I'd better be careful with that old coot.*

I spent the rest of the day poring over dusty manuscripts, having managed to skim through all four of them. I couldn't finish even one, and I moved from one to the other, unable to get beyond 50 pages of each. One was a saga about three generations of a family in Trichi, the other a poorly-plotted murder mystery, a badly-written campus romance using English words jumbled into sentences that meant nothing, and another a collection of angry rants on politics, the government, cricket, Bollywood and the state of roads in India.

After a quick sandwich at a small café downstairs, I moved to discuss the backlist with Mr Samuel, a slightly overweight, mild-mannered grandpa who looked at me with some apprehension.

'See young man, I have to leave at 3. Quickly ask me what you want.'

'Er… well, could you give me the list of books in print? Can I see the copies as well?'

'Here, take this register. There is a catalogue here. You can go to the storage and take a look at the titles. Take the keys from Sita. There are some boxes there. When we get orders from our distributor, we send the copies to him.'

'And how often do these orders come in?'

'Oh, I don't know...maybe every four to six months. They send a guy with a list of what they want, and we give them what's available. Now I have to leave; it's time for my bus,' he said, before getting up and rushing out with his office bag and a newspaper.

I could hear old Hindi music playing in Mr Kalim's cabin. Maybe I'll ask the old man to let me look at the collection of stories or the other book by Vinod Dutta.

I stood up, walked towards his cabin and knocked softly. 'Sir doesn't want to be disturbed,' Sita said icily.

'Oh, I'm sorry! When could I have a word with him, you think?'

'Maybe tomorrow, not now,' she retorted in a shrill voice, without looking up from her magazine.

I went back to my little desk in the corner of the room and began reading one of the children's adventures by Vinod Dutta. *So this was it—the unwanted editor of this redundant magazine! I've got to stick it out here till Angus sets things up, as he promised, or maybe I'll find something else. Maybe, I can start looking for a job in a magazine or as a book critic in a newspaper.*

'Mr Akshay, please come here quickly!' I looked up to see Sita from across the room. She looked upset and worried. I walked towards her and noticed tears running down her cheeks.

'He isn't moving, I think he's dead. Oh my god, it's taken him finally! This is his third heart attack,' she said hysterically, as she opened the door to his cabin.

Mr Kalim sat back in his chair with his eyes open, his arms hanging loosely by his side, dead to the world as the retro beats from the '70s played on. I stepped into the room and turned off the radio, before I shut his eyelids and requested the sobbing Sita to call an ambulance.

Leaving old Kalim with Sita, who cried as if she'd lost a member of her family, I walked over to my desk, sat back and placed a call to London. Angus picked up on the first ring.

'He's dead, mate.'

'What?! Who? Your dad? I thought the old man was fine and preparing to run a marathon.'

'Not my dad. Kalim! A massive heart attack, I reckon. What do you want to do?'

'Bloody hell! You don't say.' Angus, although taken aback initially, sounded calm and promised to take a flight to India in the coming week.

'Say mate, why don't you take over and manage things till I get there?'

'I could, but I don't think it's possible, given how this place runs. I'll wait till you get here. Sooner will be better.'

After an ambulance took Mr Kalim away with a wailing Sita in tow, I walked down and noticed scores of people staring in my direction, some out of curiosity and most with apparent disdain, like I was to blame for what had happened.

Great! First day on the new job, and my boss is dead. What's next? I thought as I got into a taxi and left for my paying guest accommodation in Colaba.

Day 14

$\mathcal{A}$ngus finally showed up two weeks after Iqbal Kalim's sudden demise, arriving well after the big funeral and the elaborate rituals and prayer meetings that followed over the past few days. He kept a low profile, however, as he wanted to stay out of the picture and fend off the press and authors who poured into office to pay their condolences. Obituaries were written; many writers and old-timers remembered the great man with kind words and sugar-coated memories of their times with him. His circle of author-friends made the office their hangout for a week. Each day was a repeat of stories from Kalim's heydays from the '70s and the '80s—a time when Iqbal Kalim was the big daddy of Indian publishing in English. A junior minister showed up to pay his condolences to Sita. Zorah Kalim, who was the sole surviving family member, the daughter of Iqbal Kalim, was often spoken about but not seen in office. There were hushed whispers about Kalim's alleged affair with Sita more than 20 years ago that broke his marriage and brought upon his downfall from the heights of success and resulted in a strained relationship with his only child.

Mr Samuel ignored everything that was happening around

him—from sobbing old writers to heartfelt tributes from Iqbal Kalim's old friends in the press. All of this left him unfazed and he ignored the presence of media and minor celebrities in the office. For the first couple of days, he furiously pored over bills and registers and carried out a stock count. The next day, he went back to his newspaper and daily routine.

Sita, however, played the helpless, heartbroken woman with aplomb. 'What will I do without him?' she asked everyone who came to pacify her. Tea, biscuits, lunch, pakoras and jalebis were sent up for her every day by the neighbours downstairs through a street kid named Munna. I was either ignored by the mourning party or looked at with deep-seated resentment. The murmur was that I had showed up on the morning of his untimely demise, called Iqbal Kalim to account and pressurized him, with support from my bosses in the UK. I overheard a jobless writer tell another: 'After a heated argument with that fellow he collapsed.' Fortunately, most of them stayed away from me, except the building watchman, Mohan Singh, who wore a deep grimace and seemed ready to pounce whenever he set his eyes on me.

Angus played it cool on entering the office. Being the smooth operator he was, he brought with him a portrait of Iqbal Kalim standing by the London Bridge in his younger years and had it hung up on a wall by the entrance. He called all of us into the meeting room and spoke gravely about how great Iqbal Kalim was, and how he could never be replaced. Mr Samuel, with a frown on his face, stood there along with Munna, who had assumed employment in the firm, and Sita wept copious tears, to Angus's visible discomfort. He went on to give a pep talk about Kalim's great future, the time for infusion of new blood into the business and how we must all work together in the memory of Iqbal Kalim and make his soul proud. He was so good—he sounded half-sincere—that I nearly believed his sentimental bullshit. Munna looked confused and grinned at him as he scratched his head; Mr Samuel looked forlorn, possibly fearing that he would be fired, and seemed as if he wanted to rush back to his newspaper, and Sita looked painfully despondent. Angus dismissed everyone asking them to continue their good work but stopped me from leaving the cabin behind the rest of them.

'Phew, that was difficult. Such an odd bunch of characters,' he said, rubbing his brow with a tissue paper.

'They certainly are. Not quite the bunch you need to run a publishing firm.'

'Yeah, gosh, it's a mess! I say, mate, I'm a little uncomfortable that we're employing underage kids. Shouldn't he be in school? That unkempt little ruffian, what's his name? Mannu?' Angus said.

'Munna, he's not employed here but seems to hang around and do the odd jobs. His mum works in the building.' *It seems like he does more work than anyone else in this office.*

'Is it? Maybe I should do something and put him in a school. It's a little strange having him work here, don't you think? There would most certainly be a scandal in the UK if it ever got out. The rags would get their knives out for my father.'

'Er…yes, probably. What do you have in mind for the future?'

'Ah yes, coming to that right away. With the old man six feet under, things actually seem promising. See Akshay, India holds tremendous promise as a market for the future. There's more spending power, more people who want to read English literature. We have a perfect situation now. We have a capable editor in you, and I've just headhunted a sales guy. He's a fairly senior management executive who'll join next week as the CEO of Kalim. He's had a decade of sales experience, and we need people who can sell and get things done.'

I looked at him with some scepticism. 'You're right, but it takes more than that. We need to evaluate and pick manuscripts. You need some capabilities in marketing and maybe even a publicist like you have in the UK. I mean, all we have is an old guy and Kalim's mistress from the past.'

'Well, here's the thing. Old Kalim has a daughter, Zorah. As per the terms we had agreed or with Kalim, after his passing, we were to recruit Zorah into the firm and keep his assistant, Sita, employed at a certain pay. Now, this daughter is working at an advertising agency and after some cajoling and a significant increase in pay, she has agreed to join us. She didn't quite get along with her dad but she could use the money and is happy to move. So she'll be here next month.' *Great, first his sobbing ex-girlfriend who doesn't do any more than sip tea and varnish her nails, and now his daughter joins in the fun too.*

'But what is she going to do? What can she do?'

'I reckon that you could hand the marketing and publicist's role to her. She's young, a twenty-something, and she's eager to work and learn. But you'll have to do a lot more. You have a role to handle the entire publishing side of things, and you have just Sita to assist you while she assists Tarun, the new CEO.'

'Handling the entire editorial team is a lot for one person, particularly if you want this business to grow. There isn't even a website or a stated process to accept submissions.' *Sita assisting me, yeah right!*

'Mate, you'll have to get that done quickly. There's no money, there's about a year's cash that my old man is throwing in to turn this ship around. If it doesn't happen, this place will have to fold,' he said with a shrug and a nod of the head.

'What choice do I have, with my back against the wall?'

'Perk up, you have two new people coming in soon. You can get it done. Go out and understand what people are reading. We need at least five books on the bestseller lists this year. This will give us a reason to go on.' He gave me one of his cunning smiles that said, 'I'm sorry but you're fucked.'

'You're setting some really challenging targets there. I've only just gotten here; there isn't a flow of manuscripts and the last book was published two years ago.'

'You'll find a way. And mate, you get this done and I can convince Dad about the literary eBooks imprint you wanted to start up with us. I feel it's a real possibility for you to move back to London and lead this new project in a year, but only if...' He sat back looking smug and knew that he had me in a tight spot, with very little elbow room to negotiate anything.

'I'll do what I can,' I said, relieved to hear about these possibilities. *This is why I am here. I have to find my way back to London. Find those five books, get some quick wins and get the hell out of here.*

'Let's go and get a beer, mate, I want to get out of this office. This seems like quite a rough neighbourhood,' Angus said.

'Yes, let's go. I could definitely use a drink,' I said, walking out of the door with Angus following in my lead.

'Angus, what's the story with this Mr Samuel? He comes in for half a day and doesn't seem to get much done. He's a bit too old to continue, don't you think?'

'He doesn't actually work here or get paid. He actually stopped getting paid some five years ago, as Kalim couldn't afford to pay him. He keeps coming in though,' Angus shrugged. 'He, apparently, ran a huge bookstore that went out of business like a decade ago. He happens to be an old associate of Iqbal Kalim and he comes in here to feel useful and while away his time. He has kids who are well off, but he doesn't like sitting at home.'

'Well, that's kind of him then, we could use an extra hand when there's more work.'

'For sure, he's a free resource; you guys have one year, mate. You've got to make it happen.' *Yeah, easier said than done! Where do I begin?*

Day 31

To celebrate my one eventful month in office, we had both Tarun and Zorah showing up for their first day at work. The office was abuzz with activity. Tarun, a portly, balding middle-aged sales manager, brought furniture for his cabin that included a chair with better ergonomics, a table lamp and some paintings of scantily clad women for the wall, which replaced pictures of Iqbal Kalim with former prime ministers and great writers, thus reducing Sita to the weeping widow once again.

Zorah, a perky, tough-as-nails, attractive brunette dressed in formal attire, made a quieter entry and quickly set up her desk on the opposite end from Sita, whom she chose to ignore. She walked up to me, while I stood watching Sita argue with Tarun about throwing away certain things from Iqbal Kalim's cabin. An IT guy had been called in to set up three laptops for Tarun, Zorah and me, and he watched on with amusement as Sita shouted and pleaded to let things be as they were.

'You're the dude from London, right?' *I like those smouldering eyes.*

'Yeah, that's me. Akshay Mathur.'

'Hi, I'm sure you know who I am. Do you want to go down

for a smoke? This place is already getting to me,' she said in her raspy voice, as she eyed me with interest.

'Sure,' I said and walked out quietly behind her. Mr Samuel didn't look too happy with the entry of new people. This meant that he could no longer read his four daily newspapers in peace.

I watched her with interest, as she had an air of confidence and clearly held her own. 'I'm sorry about your loss.'

'Well, I'm not. He wasn't much of a father,' she said with disinterest and an air of nonchalance. 'So, what's your story?' she asked as she lit up downstairs.

'I moved here from London recently.'

'Fuck you! To work at this dump?'

'Well, it's an interesting challenge to turn around a once popular publisher.'

'Ha ha! Sure. Turn around my Dad's sunken ship! I'm not a 12 year old. Even the 12 year olds these days won't buy that crap. Why are you here?' she asked. *A thinking hottie, not bad.*

'Well, for starters, I got fired recently and around the same time got divorced too. I'm broke and don't have too many options.'

'Hmm… That sounds more like why you'd be here.'

'So, what made you join this place? I hear that you and the old man weren't quite on the best terms.'

'That we weren't. Well, I could use the higher pay, for one. It's a lot better than doing client servicing and having stoned copywriters check me out all day, or have middle-aged, loser clients trying to grab my ass at their parties.'

My phone buzzed at that moment. It was Tarun calling to check where we were. 'I'm coming down, let's go out for lunch and talk,' he said before hanging up.

'Oh! He's coming down, is he? That creep!'

'Yeah, he's our boss now. We should try to get along.' I looked at her questioningly.

'Yeah right! I'll get along with him fine if he looks at my face when he's talking to me. Pervert!'

I stood there uncomfortably, smoking my cigarette as she went on about the Tarun-kind-of guys who were everywhere in India, before Tarun himself interrupted us with his toothy grin.

'My new team! *Kuch* Indian *ho jaye*?' He stared at Zorah with a wolfish grin, and she looked irritable in his presence.

'Sure,' I said and gazed at Zorah, who looked away and nodded slightly.

He drove us down to a North Indian dhaba close to the mall, a place that he frequented in his days as a sales manager. Throughout the way, he spoke to Zorah, asking her intimate questions about herself and her plans for the future.

Later, after a heavy meal at the dhaba, Tarun sat back and burped loudly.

'*Haan*, now Akshay, so how many books we have to publish?' *What, this guy, who can't frame a correct sentence, is to be my boss in a publishing business?*

'You mean how many do we have to publish? Or how many we have lined up on a publishing list? These are two different things,' I said, looking offended by his lack of table manners. Zorah sniggered, and it was obvious that both of us had little affection for this schmuck in a cheap suit.

'No no, how many you already have that we can print? You know what I mean,' he grinned awkwardly. *No, I fucking don't.* He looked agitated and hailed a waiter to get him an ice cream and another cola.

'Well, if you ask me, we have a clean slate. There's nothing we have that's worth being published.'

'No no, that's not good. You need to find something quickly, yaar. We only have one year to prove ourselves. In fact, one month has already passed. We need a lot of books; maybe some love stories, dramas…'

'We've only just set up a website to receive submissions. I suggest that we use social networking too.'

'Hmm…I'm going to ask around and find some books that we can run with. Maybe we can get some names from people working in some other publishing firms. I have contacts, na.' He burped, and a moment later, began to pick his teeth.

'Yes, those that are worth publishing. They have to stand for something, the writing, at least, has to be logical.'

'Forget all that, yaar! We need books that sell.' Zorah watched on with an amused look on her face as Tarun and I squared off. *What are we into? Selling shampoo and dog biscuits?*

'Zorah, you must have friends, na? People who write books? Mostly girls are writing all these love stories from campus and about their first sex experience.' He gave her a knowing smile, bringing a deep frown on her face.

'No, not really, I don't know anyone writing about these experiences, Tarun!'

'Really? You should do something too. Spread the word about us; ask around from those you know. We need some books quickly,' he said with some aggression.

'I'll do what I can, Tarun,' she said to shut him up, as he turned to concentrate on a spoonful of vanilla ice cream.

'Let's get back; we have a lot of work. We don't have even a single book that we could take to the market,' he said, looking at me with disappointment.

Day 40

$\mathcal{A}$nother pleasant Monday evening when I have to listen to, 'We're running out of time.' I also have to repeat my answer to the question asked every morning: 'How many books have we commissioned?' *Zero, nil, nothing, nada.*

Tarun stood before me sporting his Homer Simpson tie and his cheesy grin. 'Say, Akshay, how about if you contact some people who work in the other publishing firms?'

'And?' *Talk to them about what? The weather in Delhi?*

'Get some inside dope, yaar. Find out about writers who aren't happy or who've been rejected or have fought with their publisher. We can sign on some of these people.'

'I don't think editors give out this information to people they don't really know.'

'Maybe we can give them some incentive? Even get a few promising manuscripts passed on…'

'What do you mean?' *This doesn't smell good.*

'Well, *rokda*, extra income they say. Something that keeps them going on the side.'

'You're talking about bribing people in rival firms? I'm not going to play any part in that!'

'Yaar, this is India. You need some information, you have to find a way to get it from your competitor. It's called market research, there are agencies who specialize in this.'

'It's not a practice I would follow. Look, we are beginning to get manuscripts and I'm reading them. Let's see what comes out of it.'

'We need something quickly. I want you to sign on your first author in one week,' he retorted sharply, before walking back to his cabin. He seemed to be growing increasingly impatient, given that he had little to do apart from meeting certain distributors and retailers, and twiddle his thumbs the rest of the time.

Zorah, in a pastel dress that showed off her curves and her beautifully tanned legs, walked up to me as I was packing up to leave for the day.

'Rough day?' she smiled.

'Yeah, the usual horrid submissions. And Tarun is a delight to work with.'

She grinned, 'Aww…poor baby! Do you want to go for a drink?' I noticed the spark in her oh-so-intense eyes and smiled back at her.

'Well, I could use one. Hard Rock?'

'Fuck no! Let's go to Leopold's. Closer to your place and mine, and cheaper.'

'Sure.'

A couple of hours later, after both of us had downed a couple of drinks without saying much, she leaned in. 'What is your problem?'

'What do you mean?'

'You're so high-strung, like some protector of the sanctity of the English language. You need to loosen up, look around you.'

'I can't cheapen my standards. I have my convictions and I'm not going to sell out.'

'Hold your convictions for books that you pay for. People read to relax and unwind, very few have the time for the books that you want to publish.'

'People can watch movies to relax and unwind,' I said mimicking her tone. 'Books serve a higher purpose.'

'God! You're like my father. Like you are superior to everyone! Get over it. Did you see where he was when he died? Just take a look around you. Get real. These people work like slaves all week—they ride the local trains, eat street food. Give them a fucking break! They want to be entertained and not awestruck by well-crafted paras of prose.'

'What do you want me to do?'

'Understand what people want—like my dad did, more than 40 years back—when Kalim was at its peak. Just like the decades gone by, people are looking for simple, interesting stories that are easy to read. Try and give them just that.'

'Hmm…' I ordered another beer. 'I don't think I'm at the right place. This is just too difficult. I'm not from here, I can't relate to it and I have no clue what people want.'

'This doesn't mean you publish books that you like, books which talk down to the very people you say you don't understand! Anyway, here, this is the phone number of Tamanah, a childhood friend. She's an avid reader and will be happy to read and give you opinion on books. Like three to four books a week—you can weed out the trash and send her anything that's well written.'

'She's doing this because?' I took the number reluctantly and stared at the little Post-it.

'She's a friend, and she loves to read.'

'Thanks!'

'Yeah, I'd like you to get started. It'll give me some work to do. You need a change of tactic. Read the reviews and feedback on Amazon for your own book.'

I was taken aback—she'd taken time to research about me. 'Yeah, it's scathing. This is why I'm slumming it here.'

'I'm not surprised. Don't mess this job up like that book, else we'll all get fired.'

'I'll definitely try not to,' I said, which brought a smile to her face.

'I have another friend who works for this IT company. Now this guy's boss is a maverick entrepreneur, Sudhir. He's writing some sci-fi novel which has been turned down by quite a few publishers.'

'Okay.'

'I think we should meet him and work something out. The fact that he owns the company and is loaded will mean that he can get the book off the shelves real fast.'

'But going and meeting an author? Soliciting manuscripts? I'm not used to this.'

'These are desperate times, Akshay. They call for desperate measures.' It struck me then that I had to sign up an author in a week. Who better than a guy who can get his book sold in the marketplace?

'Okay, maybe you can set it up.' I noticed the bar getting busier and people of all ages and ethnicities starting to pour in.

'That's good. We'll try and meet him next week. There's a graphic designer kid who's coming in tomorrow to see us. He's a friend from the agency and is very creative. I was thinking of using him for book covers.'

'Good, that's interesting! We do need someone.'

'Hey, Akshay, I have this idea that I wanted to run past you.'

'Sure, go ahead.'

'We have so many old titles—classic romance novels, short stories and children's books. Why don't we repackage these in a new avatar and re-launch them? It's what companies do in food and beverages. They change the package and call it "new and improved".'

'This is a wonderful idea!' *Why didn't I think of it?*

'Yeah, and it will get Tarun off our backs for a bit, as he'll get involved selling these titles.'

'Yeah, let's go for it. Thanks, Zorah! You've been kind.'

'Oh stop with your thank yous, etc. I like you, AK; you're a pretty nice guy. I just hope we succeed with everything we do.' She leaned in and kissed me on my cheek softly before we paid and walked out of the bar, a little tipsy.

Day 47

 $\mathcal{A}$ nother day at the office going through the pages of a poorly edited copy, written by an MBA student, waiting for the day to bloody end. I was on Page 46, and I struggled to stay awake. The author was Tarun's son's friend who claimed to be a 'born writer'. I had thought that after accepting Sudhir's book, Tarun would lay off me for a while, but I was wrong. I got a call from Tarun, who incidentally sat in a cabin across the room from mine.

'Can I see you for five minutes, sir?'

Ah! He's excessively polite, I've got to be unrelenting. 'Sure, your office or mine?'

'If you can come over it will be better…'

'I'll be there.' I walked over, wondering what this was about. Another workshop on whether our logo should be in red or in green? Or whether we should have our profile shots or sketches on the 'About Us' web page?

I walked in to see him grinning at his laptop screen. *Must be porn, what else?*

'Come, come, Akshay, *baithiye* sir,' he beamed.

'Thanks, so what is it that you want to discuss?' After all, I was dying to go back to the wonderful manuscript I was evaluating.

No, I wasn't. But I didn't want to sit there and discuss colours and sizes of the company's logo. *I'd rather be in a bar somewhere. Zorah seems to be away today. Hmm…*

'So, I was wondering what your thoughts were on Roshan Khan's autobiography?' He leaned in with a grin plastered on his face. *'Thoughts', not decision? After all, I am the damn editorial director!*

I leaned back in my chair while the monkey in a suit continued giving me his smug grin.

'Without sounding disrespectful, I think it's something that should never get published. I haven't seen such drivel in my life. It's a self-indulgent piece of work by a narcissistic…'

'He is one of the biggest stars in this country. Such a big name, you know? With a phone call or two, he can have the biggest in the business lining up to publish his book. He and I go back a long way, the days when he used to endorse Winter Chill energy drinks.' *Sure, moron! Winter Chill energy drinks don't exist any more, thanks to your wonderful strategy.*

'Be as it may, I can't stand for this kind of writing to be published. We are into publishing literature and not an advertorial or PR piece for Bollywood stars…'

'Well, okay-ji, point taken. Don't get upset Akshay, *hota hai*. This is India yaar, you have to adjust, you see.'

I didn't see, and I never would. I left his cabin more agitated and confused than I had been.

I wrote him a terse one-liner also marked to Sita and Zorah that went:

'Further to our discussion, I request you to kindly decline Mr Khan's biography. I haven't read such an asinine piece of work in my life and I'm definitely not in this job to publish this quality of content. I wish him good luck in finding a publisher who will be excited at the prospect of working with a respected star such as himself.'

Two hours later, while I was falling asleep at my desk reading yet another love story, a rather obsessive one, set in an engineering college, I heard a knock on my door. It was Roshan Khan standing there with a bunch of cronies and his trademark smirk.

Great! He's here to either fight or haggle with me. I opened the door to shake his hand and got a hug from the man instead. The flashbulbs went off. Most of these guys weren't his cronies but cameramen from leading newspapers. He wore a simple polo T-shirt and a pair of designer jeans. *What is he up to?*

'Get one more of me and my new publisher, Mr Ashmit,' he said to a photographer.

'Mr Akshay,' I said firmly, and looked at him with searching eyes. I wondered what was happening. He turned his gaze away and continued smiling for the shutterbugs, with one arm around my shoulder.

After the photo-op, he turned to his publicist, Archana. 'Put up one of the good publisher and I on Twitter,' he quipped.

He walked into my cabin uninvited and made himself at home.

'You really need to redecorate your office. Get some art on the walls, sex up the place a little bit. Maybe I can get you a painting or two we can pitch that to the papers as a PR piece too. I can put my wife on the job; she does this for celebrity homes. For you, I can waive off her fees,' he said with his cocky smile. *Nice, this is the prize I get for sitting through his self-indulgent rambling.*

I had reached the ebb of my limited patience. 'And how can I help you?' Over his shoulders, I saw Tarun walk swiftly towards my cabin, with Zorah a few steps behind him. She looked at me with a sigh. *Back to earth, big boy, you have trouble sitting before you.*

'Thanks for agreeing to publish my book,' he said effusively. You had to give it to the man, he was charm personified. At that moment, Tarun walked through the door giving me a thumbs up.

'Welcome to Kalim Publishing, Mr Khan! It's our privilege to publish the autobiography of a great actor,' he said. *What the... !*

'No, no, I should thank you,' he said with a humble smile. 'I was touched when Tarun called saying that you loved the book, and that it moved you to tears,' he said turning towards me. He beamed at me while I turned to nod at Zorah, who walked in. *Moved to tears, of course. Tears of frustration for having to sit through such a load of crap.*

'I...'

'We are very excited about your book, Mr Khan,' Tarun said, putting his arm around the big shot's back. Zorah gave me a searching gaze that said, 'What are they talking about?' I had spent the last evening with her, over a few mugs of beer at Leopold's, where I tore the book to pieces as she listened with rapt attention.

The star was busy staring at the screen of his Porsche Design phone while Tarun had jealous eyes trained on his pair of Armani glares.

'Your last film, *Khan is King,* was superb, sir! Too good,' Tarun said excitedly, spitting out his words and gesticulating like a circus monkey.

'*Haan haan*, the critics have really praised me, hai na? Tarun Bhai, *chalo* next time. I hope I still win all the awards', he said with a wink. *Sure, you can dance at the award's night and take home that dumb trophy, you moron.*

'This will be a big news item in tomorrow's paper,' he said proudly. 'So Zorah, I really look forward to working with you,' he said, before tugging her arm and giving her a tight hug. *What's with this hugging business?*

'Sure,' she said with a wry grin and made eyes at me.

'We have to sit down, you know, plan the marketing and the launch. I'd like this done properly, so we should start with a press conference where we can make a formal announcement.'

'Yes, Mr Khan, we'll be in touch,' she said.

'Well yes, let's do coffee tonight at JW Marriott and chat,' he grinned.

'I'm afraid that won't be possible, as I have other plans. How does tomorrow 10 a.m. at our office work?' She stood with arms crossed and a polite smile, while Tarun looked shifty and began to sweat, as her rebuke wiped the smile off the superstar's face.

'I'll have to get going, please talk to Venkat, my manager,' he said, flashing his cocky smile. *And women swoon over this? Damn!*

'Sure, I will,' she said.

'So, I trust you'll make some editorial suggestions and comments; I look forward to them,' he said, turning his attention to me.

'Yes, that's how it's done, isn't it? We'll be in touch.'

He sauntered out with a nod, while Tarun stayed back giving a sheepish smile.

'I had said I didn't want to publish this book,' I fumed.

'He's one of the biggest stars. It's a done deal; look at the attention it will bring us. We need it,' he said, flashing his crooked yellow teeth.

'But we need to stand for a certain quality, an honesty which this book fails to depict in any sense.'

'Well, you can edit it a bit. We are getting Supercon Appliances and YL Jeans to do a product placement deal. This means we are publishing the book at no cost to us.'

'But is this the direction we're supposed to head in?' Zorah asked, sounding less than pleased with his decision.

'We don't have a choice. We need to survive—at least I do,' he said, turning to frown at me before storming out of my cabin.

'Fucking buffoon!' I said, as I paced up and down the room. Zorah sat down on the couch, staring across the hallway at her father's portrait.

Sita and Mr Samuel looked star-struck. What happened today was unlike anything they had seen in the years that Kalim Publishing limped on through its dreary existence.

We heard a knock on the door and the superstar's publicist popped her head in. 'Ms Kalim, Mr Khan has requested you to please join him outside the building. He is talking to the press and is getting pictures taken.'

'Sure, I'll be there in a minute,' she said, standing up to leave.

'Well, Tarun is right about this… It's good publicity for us. The last time we had a mention in the papers was when Dad passed away,' she said reluctantly, as she walked towards the door. 'I don't think you should fight Tarun on this one. Let go, this is good for us,' she said, before she sauntered across the hallway and out of the office. I couldn't help but admire her shapely figure as she headed towards the elevator across the hallway. Deciding to rest my eyes and get away from my laptop for a while, I randomly pulled out one of the manuscripts old Kalim had left behind. It was a collection of essays called *Bottled Up* by two people—Sandeep, a Left-leaning Economics graduate from St Stephens, and Shipra, a former Greenpeace activist. I began skimming through it and soon was sucked in. I was amazed by the honesty and belief the authors had in everything they wrote about. I started making notes, and sent out a long memo to the authors, before I sat back and pondered the essays on tribal displacement, environmental degradation and poaching of jungle cats till it was half past ten, and a coy Zorah was in the cabin, softly whispering into my ear that it might be a good idea to go and get something to eat before she could let me take her back to her place.

Day 63

And so, it continues. I'm put under increasing pressure from Tarun to commission more books for publishing. He even picked up the phone and ranted off to Angus about me being uppity and high-strung with Indian authors. An aged author complained that I refused to give her time for her upcoming novel. *A romance set in the pre-Independence days that was a rehash of a number of films set in that era.*

It didn't help matters that the old lady's son was a senior Congress minister. *Yeah, and I have to deal with the 'you know who you're talking to' shit.* Thankfully, though, the old lady went to another publisher who knew exactly who they were talking to and managed to get a sweet publishing deal. It was also pointed out to Angus that I was less than friendly to Roshan Khan, who offered to let me use his gym and work out with him. 'I don't fancy the idea of waking up at 6 a.m. and working out,' I had said. So, I'd been told to be as friendly and open-minded as possible. Except that, Angus didn't put it so politely.

Tarun entered my cabin to needle me as usual. He looked like a donkey showing his yellow teeth proudly.

'That Angus is very hot-headed, hai na?'

'Yeah, that's how we talk to each other. I've known him for years.' Indians abuse each other regularly. The closer you are, the more Hindi *gaalis* are hurled at you. It's a sign of affection. I tried to pass off Angus's tirade with that excuse. In no way was I going to let Tarun have the pleasure of seeing me worked up.

'I couldn't take such insults, *hain*? I would say, "goodbye ****iya", and leave.' *Ah, provocation.*

'Yeah, I think he's a nice guy. Very upfront and direct sometimes, but that's okay. It's better than dealing with manipulative bastards who play games behind your back.'

'Hmmm…,' he said, looking away and grinning nervously.

'They have no guts, mate. I found out about one such guy who tried to mess with me in my last job in London.'

'What happened?'

'The asshole was telling my boss that I used to sneak away in the afternoon for a drink.'

'What did you do?' he stood with his hands defiantly on his hips.

'I blew out all four tyres of his car. I cut them with a knife.'

'Ha ha ha…'

'Then I stabbed him in the men's room of a pub a few nights later, when he was taking a piss. The best thing is that they never found out. It happens every day in London. What's that phrase you use, hmm, *chalta hai*?' I laughed manically, like the villain Mogambo from a Bollywood film I'd seen.

'What are you saying, yaar?' He took two steps back, almost ready to rush out of the door, watching me grin wickedly.

'Tarun!'

'Yes?'

'Don't tell anyone. I have this amazing collection of butcher's knives. I can show you one day.'

'Yaar, let's talk later. I have to go for a meeting.' He rushed out of the cabin and walked hurriedly towards the restroom. *Let's hope that keeps him out of my hair for a while.*

Taking a break from the adventures of a former Indian naval officer in Samoa, I took out my copies of newspapers that I had picked up from the stand downstairs. In keeping with Angus's instructions to understand things around me, I must be aware of the happenings in the city.

Flipping through the papers quickly, I got to the last page of the *Mumbai Times*, and a very interesting story caught my attention—'Publisher finds mentor in Roshan Khan'. The article spoke at great length about how Roshan Khan was helping me redo my apartment, working out with me, giving me tips on yoga and healthy eating, and helping me get off the booze; apparently, he had even bought me a watch and a new iPhone. It waxed eloquent about how kind and generous Roshan had been since my move from London and how he had helped me feel at home in Mumbai. I felt like throwing up my breakfast. I crushed the last page of the newspaper before I threw it into the bin. *Son of a bitch!*

I opened the *Mid-Afternoon* to read another interesting piece of gossip. 'Spotted: Editor/Writer Akshay Mathur, who was loading up on DVDs of Roshan Khan's films. The young publisher is a big fan of Roshan Khan, whose autobiography his troubled firm, Kalim, will publish in a few months. Will this help them out of the muddy waters?' *Oh, fuck me!*

My phone rang just then. 'Akshay, what's up, my brother? Paper *dekha* na?'

'Yes!'

'You must be happy. You've become a Page 3 celebrity,' Roshan said with his trademark snigger.

'It really isn't ....'

'Listen brother, there's this party tomorrow night at Director Ramesh Bhatia's place. It's the old bastard's eighth wedding anniversary of his second marriage. You should come with me. A couple of popular British directors are also coming. We'll make an entrance together, the media will be there.'

'I don't even know the guy.' *I bet he's another schmuck who sucks up to you. Or is it the other way around?*

'Arey, don't worry na! He's a brother. It will be a great publicity stunt for the book, and I'm angling for this part as an Englishman in a film. I'll send my driver around to pick you up. And, I'll be sending you a suit and a Rolex watch tonight—things the papers will say I've gifted you.'

'Thank you!' I said with as much sarcasm as I could.

'Mention not, brother! It's good having a buddy who reads and everything. The last time I read a book was back in school.' *I can see that, you chump! It must've been third grade.*

'Yeah ...'

'And you went to Cambridge too. You're an intelligent guy. Be with me and you'll become famous. We can help each other. Hai na? See you tomorrow.'

'Yes, tomorrow. Bye now.' *I quit! I fucking quit!*

Noticing the grimace on my face from a distance, Zorah came knocking.

'Khan again, huh?'

'Yeah,' I said, devoid of energy.

'Hmm ... it's past 9. It's a Friday evening, let's get out of here.'

'I have to make an appearance with him tomorrow.'

'Damn! Do you want to go and get a beer?'

'Hell yeah!'

After six beers each at Leopold's, through which I whined about putting up with Roshan Khan and Tarun's antics, and Zorah about her father and Tarun, I walked her back to her little apartment near Colaba Causeway. I took the stairs up to her apartment and went in for a cup of coffee, which both of us were too wasted to make. We ended up making love on her little bed instead. At first, it was frenzied and laboured; I fumbled with her clothes before I yanked them off and thrust myself into her, and then again slowly, an hour later, when I undressed her and caressed her breasts, kissing her softly as she got on top of me and moaned with pleasure till she came. We fell asleep in each other's arms on the mattress on the floor, and woke up with my first hangover in India, but with a big smile, watching Zorah, wearing nothing but her underwear, sleeping like a baby with her arm around me. She pinned me down and refused to let me get out of bed. Instead, we cuddled and wrestled for a while, before I sprang up to make some coffee and toast, and she shyly reached out for my shirt that was thrown on the floor next to the mattress. I couldn't help admiring those firm, supple breasts as I heated the milk, and she caught my eye looking at her. Buttoning up, and smiling at the ground, she walked up beside me and kissed me softly on the nape of my neck before nibbling at it playfully.

'You seem hungry. Slept well, honey?'

'Honey?' she laughed, making a face and shaking her head, showing that she abhorred the name. 'Yeah, I did. What about you?' She made eyes at me and licked her luscious lips.

'Indeed, I did.'

'You fucking Englishman! Acting all proper the morning after. You were pretty good,' she said, playfully gazing into my eyes as I wrapped my arms around her.

'You weren't too bad yourself. You're quite an aggressive one, huh? Look at the scratches,' I said, showing the work she'd done on my torso. I was sure my back was worse.

'Yeah, you deserve it,' she smirked.

'What now?'

'Breakfast.'

'And then?'

'Maybe a nice, hot shower?' *Man, I'm in love with this little vixen.*

'Ah-huh, and what do you propose we do after that?' I asked, as I played with her hair.

'I don't know, maybe go back to bed,' she said while she removed the plates and I admired her rack not too obviously.

'Stop acting all proper and discreet after all we got up to last night.'

'I was…'

'Ssshhh…' she said, pushing me against the wall cabinet and wrapping her legs around me.

'Breakfast can wait,' she hissed before drawing her moth-kissed lips onto mine.

Day 71

$\mathcal{I}$ walked into office with a throbbing head. I didn't recollect much of what had happened last night. If I remembered correctly, that morning, a pissed-off Zorah had pushed me away as I moved in to kiss her and had walked out of my apartment. I wondered what it was about. She gave me a cold stare and turned back to her laptop when I wished her that morning.

My phone buzzed continuously with alerts from Twitter. Sudhir, the man who was my first sign-up at the firm, had sent me a direct message. A bloke who was peddling an *Independence Day*-meets-*Armageddon*-meets-*Star Wars*-meets-fucking-*Gladiator* novel as his original masterpiece. A bloke who didn't email people but DM-ed them on Twitter or Inboxed them on Facebook. I refused to sign up for Facebook—or in other words a hangout for voyeurs. It was the latest thing for people to compare their lives with someone else's and constantly stay updated on what others were doing, who they were snogging and such.

I signed in to read his direct message. 'Letz plz meet 2 discuss chap. 24. Time?' *Bollocks!*

For want of a respectable editor, I had the honour of editing Sudhir's manuscript as well; there was no getting away from this one. We had agreed to publish this, given his stature as the poster boy of the internet space in India, and the desperation to get Tarun and Angus off my ass for a while. Instead, now I had someone worse than Angus, one with an obsessive-compulsive disorder—the great Sudhir. He was widely known as a maverick who'd founded two internet start-ups and had sold them for a fortune. He now spent most of his time at a beach house in Goa and occasionally came in to spend a few days at his sea-facing, 27th-floor apartment in Worli. He was often invited to lecture at business schools and as a speaker at business forums for middle-aged executives stuck in dead-end jobs.

Before I could reply to his message, I received another one. 'Whatz da plan 4 promoting ma book in NY & London?? Plz reply ASAP.' *Would you leave me in peace if I didn't?*

These days he was obsessed with this ludicrous sci-fi novel set in the future, and in us he had found a willing publisher who could be mollified into doing things his way. He was another star in the making that Tarun had gotten deliriously excited about, and I was expected to give him my undivided time and attention.

I sat down with my aching head to reply to him. I decided to call him instead, as I didn't want to start a painful exchange of messages on Twitter. He picked up the call on the first ring.

'Talk to me, Mathur,' he said in his gruff voice. I hadn't met a less polite creature in my life. No conversation of his started with asking about another person.

'Yes, how are you today?' *I'm sure the X-Box is keeping you occupied.*

'Alright. Did you read my messages?' *Sure, and I succeeded in deciphering them too.*

'Indeed, I did.'

'And?'

'Yes, why don't you come by to the office after 5 p.m., and we can talk about your chapters.' *Chapters that I had to edit and make grammatical sense of, line by line.*

'What about the launch in New York and London? These are huge markets for my writing...' *Writing? More likely heaps of techno garble.*

'It may be worthy to engage Zorah in this discussion, as she handles marketing...'

'I sent her a message on WhatsApp, she hasn't replied.' He sounded offended.

'When was this?'

'Four minutes ago.'

'Oh, I guess she's busy in a meeting; I can see her phone lying on her desk. It isn't with her,' I lied. She hated him, and couldn't stand his attitude.

'Why don't you liaise with her? The three of us can have a web conversation on this. Or we could do a three-way chat on Skype?'

'Why don't you come in this evening and we'll rope her into our discussion?'

'Can't we do this earlier?' *Sure, I have nothing to do but play Pokemon all day.*

'I'm afraid I have meetings set up for the rest of the day, and I'm sure she's tied down too.'

'Hmm...well okay, I'll see you at 5.'

I hung up and walked over to Zorah, who turned around and frowned at me. She still looked stunningly beautiful and I so wanted to wrap my arms around her and kiss those luscious lips.

'Good morning,' I said, putting my arm on her shoulder. Sita had her eyes trained on us as she pretended to type, while Mr Samuel continued to read the newspaper undisturbed.

'What?' she said, recoiling with irritation.

'Sudhir has been trying to reach you…'

'I know, I saw his fucking message.'

'If you could please reply…'

'I can't keep responding to that arrogant prude. The company doesn't pay my phone bills. Please ask him to send me a polite and formal email, and I'll respond.'

'You know him…' I said, putting one hand on my head.

'Well, you know me,' she said in huff.

'Anyway, he's coming here at 5. I'm requesting you to join us.'

'Hmm… As if my day couldn't get any worse.'

I walked in to hear my phone ring. It was Vasant, the superstar's manager.

'Hi! Roshan has a request for you,' said the voice at the other end.

'Tell me.'

'He wants you to please remove the section on his friendship with the director of his first film, Vijay Kapoor.'

'It's actually one of the well-written sections of the book. I think the friendship has been brought out really well,' I responded.

'No, there is a problem. Roshan and Mr Kapoor have had a fallout. He has cast someone else in his next two films and shelved the film they had planned together. He had the nerve to tell the press that Roshan Khan doesn't fit the image of a superhero. Roshan doesn't want anything to do with him!' He sounded more outraged than Roshan Khan would himself have been.

'Okay, I'll remove the passages.' *Go eat a Valium, man, and find your boss a saas–bahu soap opera.* So much for real friendship and the man who gave him his first break in films.

Before I had put down the phone, I turned my attention to the screen. It was an email from mihin_rocks66@futuremail.com. The subject was 'my book!!!'

I clicked on the subject to open his email. I wondered how he had found out my personal email id. All manuscripts were sent to a slush pile and rejection letters went out through an editorial team email id.

Dear sir,

I send you my true love story call 'Radha'. You not reply. Why sir? Why do like this with poor fellow writer. I still waiting for reply. My book is modern love story and is written like all the bestseller in English. Myself software engineer from Softech, Madurai. My native place is Surat and I living in the Coimbatore.

Yours truly,
Mihin Mehta
B'sc 4.2 GPA

If his book was written in the same way as his wonderful letter, it deserved to be thrown into the fire.

Before I could click on delete, I received another email from him. The subject said: '…' I opened his email to see a terse one line: 'I still waiting for your reply.' *Wait, and keep doing just that, psycho!*

I hollered at Sita to come into my office. I requested her to promptly send him a polite letter declining his manuscript and wishing him luck.

A few minutes later, I had another email. I wanted to block his email address but I was curious to see what this psycho had written. I opened it. It said: 'Why you say no? My story very good. Just like all bestseller book. My Radha read and like. My all frnds also like. My father like book very much. It is first English book he read. But you don't like? Why? I wait ...'

Oh my god! This guy needs help. I signed out of my account and turned my attention to Vinod Dutta's manuscript. It was the finest bit of writing I had come across in my time with the firm so far. I had pulled it out from a dusty bundle I had found in the bottom drawer of Kalim's desk. Though it did make me squirm knowing that this was by far the most explicit passage I'd read, strewn with lurid, but graphic, details of erotic lovemaking by a once famous children's author. Naturally, it seemed very inspired by his experiences and affairs he was rumoured to have had three to four decades ago.

My phone buzzed again with a direct message from Sudhir. 'Want 2 change the setting 4m 2030 2 2045. Will make it more xciting!! Thoughts? Ideas?'

Who exactly did this guy think I was? He couldn't get through the day without sending me a dozen messages.

'Let's discuss at 5 p.m., thanks,' I responded.

I picked up the phone and dialled Mr Dutta's number.

'Hello,' he wheezed loudly at the other end.

'Mr Dutta, this is Akshay from Kalim Publishing. How are you getting on?'

'Oh Akshay! Yes, yes! Hello!'

'I wanted to talk to you about this ... err ... collection of erotic short stories you sent us.'

'Young man, you see, Iqbal never called me to discuss my work,' he said before coughing loudly.

'I see…'

'He would come down to see me, and we would sit and drink scotch together, and then talk. Why don't you come over for a drink or cup of tea, if you prefer sometime next week or maybe the week after?'

'Sure, that sounds good.'

'Let me get my diary and find a date for you. I get a few visitors, you see.'

'Sure, sir,' I said and waited for him to confirm an afternoon 12 days hence.

'Fine then… Good day, son.'

'Err… Mr Dutta.'

'Yeeess?'

'Sir, I was wondering if you really wanted us to publish this. As you know, you're such a respected children's author, while this is a genre…'

'Of course I want to publish this!' he shouted irritably before he had another coughing fit. 'It's the only thing left to be published from all that I've written,' he wheezed.

'Yes sir, I understand. I'll see you in a few days for a cup of tea.' *I'm also going to wear a hat with a bow and bring my cat for company.*

'Very well then, gentleman,' he said, before clearing his throat and banging down the receiver.

Tarun walked in without a knock. He had one of his 'I know it all' grins plastered on his face.

'Akshay, Anya Malik is coming in to see us next week,' he said with his wide grin. 'She did her last two novels with Kitaab

& Co. Her first was a national bestseller. I'm sure you have heard of *16 Forever*?'

'Well, frankly, I haven't. Was it any good?'

'Huh? 25,000 copies sold! First class!'

'Fantastic, I'm most certainly delighted to hear that.' *Why did I have to ask him?*

'The second one was okay, didn't live up to the expectations. She now plans to bounce back with the third.' I figured her ex-publisher wasn't too keen to take the plunge with that one.

'Well, we'll have a look. What is it about?'

'Whatever it is, we have to publish her. She can write anything—she's Anya Malik. Anyway, she said it was a love story set in 2025. *Aise kuch hai hi-fi.*'

'We'll see,' I said, as he gazed at me with contempt and left the room.

I got on to Google and searched for information on Anya Malik and her last two books. *Hmm… not bad, at least people know who she is. And she's written before.*

Day 82

$\mathcal{I}$ spent the morning fending off calls from the *Twilight* stars, not Robert Pattinson or Kristen Stewart, but the bunch of characters that had put together Iqbal Kalim's *Twilight* collection of stories—one he believed would help redeem the firm's reputation. I didn't think so. Sparing odd bits of promising writing, most of the prose was laboured and repetitive. I put them off saying that plans to publish this were on hold as we were still evaluating our list closely. The phone rang again.

'Hello,' I said with little enthusiasm.

'Hello, sir! This is Jagan.'

'Sorry, do I know you?'

'I am Suryakant Joshi-ji's assistant, sir. He met you at Roshan Khan's party.' *Right! The gloriously drunk former state education minister who ate my head about the art of writing.*

'Sure, how can I help?'

'He wanted to know about his autobiography, sir.'

'Well, ask him to please send it to us, and I would be happy to have a look…'

'No, no sir. It hasn't been written yet.'

'I don't get this. We don't agree to publish something unless…'

'He wants you to write it for him, and then publish it.' *Oh!*
Fuck you!

'What?'

'Yes, sir. His daughter, Baby-ji, says you are a very good
writer. You are from Oxford also.'

'I'm from Cambridge! But you can't expect me to write his
manuscript for him.' *Baby-ji? What the...*

'We will pay ₹300,000, sir.'

'I'm not sure...' *Ah, now we're talking.*

'Well, ₹450,000, sir. This is surely a good amount and our
final offer, all cash. After all, you have unpaid debt in Englaaand.'
I could picture him smiling at the other end. The bastard had
done his research on my poor credit rating. I could barely get
by on my pay and had outstanding settlements on my credit
card back in the UK.

'Okay, let's meet this weekend.'

'*Acha*, we'll pick you up for breakfast next Sunday morning,
sir; we'll go to Joshi-ji's farmhouse. Guru-ji says it's an auspicious
day to make new beginnings.' *Guru who?*

'Take down my address...'

'We know where you live. See you next Sunday,' he said,
before hanging up. I stood up; it was time to leave for tea with
the renowned Vinod Dutta.

He lived in a rundown little villa in Wadala, which was a
little away from the noise and chaos of the railway station and
the market. His caretaker, Ramu, a morose hunchback himself,
led me to a dimly-lit study where Vinod Dutta was sitting in his
reclining chair and reading a book.

'Hello, sir! It's a pleasure and an honour to meet you.' He
gazed at me with worry and then surprise.

'Hmm, yes yes. You're the fellow from Kalim, right? Boy, you're a bit too young for this aren't you?'

'I look young; I have a picture growing old somewhere.'

'Ah, Oscar Wilde! *The Picture of Dorian Gray*, isn't it? You see, boy, this is still all there.' He said tapping his head. 'It's just that I've grown weak physically. My lungs aren't going to hold up for too long,' he sighed and put his book down. I noticed a hardcover version of Anton Chekhov's collection of stories on his side table. The caretaker crept into the room with two cups of tea and a plate of cookies, and after setting it down on a centre table, crept out as quickly as he had entered.

'What do you propose to do with the book?' he asked expectantly, as he quietly sipped from his cup.

'I think it's rather good. A very good sense of place and time, well-etched characters, a very bold novel, I would say. It's the best work of fiction I've read since I've taken up this job.'

'Thank you!' he beamed. 'Do you know, boy, it's my only book that's real. It's about me, about things that happened.'

'The army officer's wife? The actress who frequented the Royal Manor in the book?'

'Yes, all people who lived, women I loved and had a relationship with. You see, we were discreet about these things in those days,' he said with a twinkle in his eyes.

'There is a lot of passion in your words…'

'Yes, and you see this book must get published. It's like an autobiography of sorts.' His eyes lit up.

'It's an erotic novel.'

'Oh! Is that what you call a book like mine these days? Come on, don't make a fuss about this now! Iqbal sat on it until he rolled off the face of the earth. Now you'll sit on it till

I'm gone six feet under.'

'We'll have to think about it.' He sat there gazing at the floor like a child whose candy had been snatched away.

'It's my best piece of work; there are memories in there, real emotions!'

'We'll do it. I have to talk to the office, but I think it's possible.' *It was likely to kick up a storm. I mean who would have imagined...*

'Really? Promise me that this will happen before I'm gone. I want to live to see this book published.'

'Yes, of course.' I looked at him carefully and said, 'but I'd like you to do something for me. It's a sort of a proposition, a trade-off, if you will.'

'What?' he said, with trepidation in his voice. I explained what I needed him to do, and he took it all in with a grim expression on his face. He sat back and smiled as he finished his tea. 'Do you want some scotch?' he asked with a broad smile. He beckoned his caretaker, who was standing by the door like an invisible man. He then turned to me and nodded his head, 'I sure as hell agree to what you have in mind.'

∎

I was back at work after a few drinks with the great author, relieved that the meeting went well. We were on course to gambling on what I had in mind. I saw Zorah bending over her desk and staring furiously at her screen.

'Hey there, muffin,' I whispered with a grin, as I leaned in behind her and patted her posterior.

'Don't!' she turned around with irritation. It had been over 10 days since she'd spoken to me outside of work. Her phone was switched off over the weekend and she refused to respond to any of my messages. 'Have you been drinking in the middle of the day?'

'No!' She looked at me with disbelief while she stood with folded arms.

'Just a glass of scotch. Actually four, or maybe five. Oh, I don't know. Who cares?'

She took my hand and pulled me into my cabin as Sita watched on with disappointment. She couldn't see the drama playing out from where she sat. Zorah sat in my place and I took a seat opposite her.

'Zo, why are you mad at me, love? You look amazing!' *I just want to…*

'Shut up AK! Can you hear yourself? It's the middle of the day!'

'We've signed up Vinod Dutta's book; I just had a couple of drinks with the old man.'

'Do you know why I've been mad at you?'

'No, and it's driving me crazy. I'm guessing you'll tell me now. Enlighten me, love…' *This is easy, she'll crib, I'll say sorry and we'll end up in the sack.*

'You drink way too much! The other night, the last time I was at your place, you smashed an old vase getting all mad about your ex-wife, and then you passed out while we were making love. The next morning you remembered nothing! You're out of control these days!'

'I'm sorry that happened. I agree that night was crazy…'

'You've got to really curb your habits. Clean up or we're done! I'm not wasting my life with an alcoholic.'

'I am not…' *Am I?*

'You look and sound like one. Now pick up your things and come home with me. You're staying with me from now, get it?'

'Yes ma'am, we'll move my stuff this weekend.' *Wait! Did she ask me to move in with her? Women! From not talking to me for ten days to commanding me to move in!*

'No, no, you're still drunk. No kissing me with that foul breath of yours!' she hissed, as I leaned in and hugged her. 'You're a jackass, you know that, don't you?'

'Yeah I am, alright? And you're such a sweetie.' I smiled at her sheepishly.

'Shut up! I'm not some 12-year-old fat girl with a lollipop.'

'Yeah, that you sure aren't.' I played with her hair and kissed her forehead. *Not a bad day! Signing up a promising erotic novel, getting Dutta to agree with my plan and getting out of the doghouse with Zorah.* We celebrated over cups of coffee that night and hit the sack early. In bed, I explained to her what was on my mind. 'That's wicked,' she beamed, before we cuddled and kissed, and she fell asleep in my arms.

Day 86

On a Sunday morning, I arose to a stinker of an article that Zorah thrust in my face, along with a cup of coffee. 'Hangers on', read the title. It listed small-time actors, failed actors, make-up artists, music composers, designers and writers, including me, with a thumbnail image to boot, who were living off leading celebrities. 'The critically acclaimed young writer whose first book was a disaster and who is now the editor of the doomed, once great publishing house, Kalim, is a fixture in Roshan Khan's entourage and is often seen sporting expensive watches and smoking cigars at the superstar's bashes.' *Oh man! Thankfully my Mum isn't in India and is not reading this.*

'You really have a reputation now, don't you?' Zorah giggled, as she ruffled my hair.

'Yeah, yeah. I also have a fake Instagram profile where the fake Roshan Khan and I comment on each other's posts all day. This is such a mess!'

'It's really funny,' Zorah chuckled, 'you being thrown in with all these losers! See, your picture is next to Ekta Khanna. She did some five flop films, then did a reality TV show; now she just hangs out at parties.'

'Yeah, it's quite a bunch of wannabes and has-beens.'

My phone rang, and I expected it to be Tarun, who would have preferred if it had been him in the papers instead of me.

'Ram Ram, Jagan here, sir.'

'Oh hello! Ram Ram, Jagan.' *Damn, I have to meet that ex-minister today.*

'Sir, I am waiting downstairs, you not come.'

'Oh, is it? See, I've moved out of that apartment a few days back. I will text you my new address.'

'Yes sir, send me sir. I will come and get you.'

I handed the phone to Zorah to text him and quickly took a shower and got ready. An hour later, I was sitting in a lawn, amongst trees and chirping birds, in Suryakant Joshi's Panvel farmhouse. He walked into the lawn, dressed in a starch white kurta pyjama, greeted me with a friendly 'namaste' and gestured me to take a seat. Two bodyguards took their positions behind his chair and Jagan brought him a heap of files that he glanced at with a nod and a slight smile.

'What do you prefer? Tea or coffee? I can tell you, tea will be better,' he said with a careful smile.

'Tea it is then, thank you.'

'Two ginger teas and the breakfast,' he told the attendant, who stood with his head bowed.

'This is a very nice place,' I said, looking around. I noticed kids, presumably his grandchildren, playing with a golden retriever and a cocker spaniel.

'It has been in our family for generations. It was a holiday home and now I more or less live here. What do I have to do in the city? I've retired from active politics.' *Politicians don't retire unless they are six feet under.*

'You're still an MLA, Mr Joshi, aren't you?'

'*Haan*, but see, this is about to end. I just want to complete the work I promised my constituency. The party isn't giving me a ticket for re-election, even though I've won six times. They want to promote youngsters now.'

'That's unfortunate...'

'Yes, I still have that drive in me to make a difference. I did so much as the education minister, and yet I was removed to accommodate that fellow from Sholapur who was our alliance partner. What did he do? He didn't even go to office and look at files.'

'Oh, that's shocking! What a waste!'

'Bah... see all these files, I opened 100 new schools in rural areas, 2,000 schools were revamped, changed the syllabus for IIT, introduced astrology as a subject in primary school...'

He launched off with a long monologue about his achievements and went on about all the great things he had done, the international seminars he had spoken at and how education was important for young minds. He also gave a bit of a flashback about his life as a teacher in a village primary school and his entry into politics when he joined the Apna Democratic Party at the behest of the now Leader of Opposition, Madan Gokhle. He did come off as someone who was well intentioned and sincere. I managed to stay awake after a heavy breakfast by watching sparrows move around on trees and the pranks his grandchildren were getting up to with the dogs, who seemed more than eager to destroy the flower beds. He then began with another story from his childhood that made me sit up and listen.

'The leader and I were friends in school and then college in Nagpur. Our families know each other for generations. He was a very fun-loving and naughty kid, and I was the good one. Later after college, as we whiled away our time every evening near the market, he set his eyes on Alisha, a girl from Kerala who was studying to become a nurse. He would make eyes at her and follow her on his bicycle. He tried to buy her samosas once and jalebis another time, but she refused. A little later, she began to give in to his advances and walked to her hostel with him. He even followed her back home to Thiruvananthapuram during a vacation. Her family got to know about it—they lived in a very small place, you see, and people talk. Her brother and his friends bashed up Gokhle Bhai and broke his arm. It led to a communal violence, as Gokhle Bhai's uncle got involved with some local troublemakers in Thiruvananthapuram and harassed the family when they were leaving church. Alisha was quickly married off to a man who worked in a shipping company in Kuwait, and she was never seen again. Gokhle Bhai was bitter and heartbroken. Very soon he joined a few other people and launched the Apna Democratic Party, which sadly has pursued a divisive agenda. He was a very nice man; it's just that his mind is filled with hate and anger for other communities and this, mind you, is misplaced and personal.'

I nodded along with rapt attention. *There* was the reason I was here and he was saying it. *There* was the reason he wanted to publish this book, not to talk about his brief stint as a minister and his journey into politics—nobody really cared about that. He had scores to settle; he was removed from his post and sidelined in favour of an illiterate, country hick. Now he was retiring, and quite obviously he was not a man in good books any more. The reasons for this were obvious. When the last chief minister in the previous ADP-led government had taken ill and seemed unlikely to return, which he did, there were strong hints that he was the front runner for the post as the next chief minister if the CM's condition deteriorated, given that he was a compromise candidate who worked well with others. As for Madan Gokhle, he was seen as a tainted man, a hardliner if you will, who was unacceptable to many even within his own party. On the other hand, Suryakant Joshi had everything going for him, a clean record, good performance, cordial relationships across party lines and was seen as an impeccable speaker with an amiable personality. With one sweeping move by the acting chief minister and his former best mate, he was removed as minister citing coalition compromises and made the speaker of the assembly, and paraded as a candidate for the presidential election two years later, when they clearly didn't have the numbers or coalition support to get him elected. Post his crushing defeat in the presidential election, he was relegated to the backbenches, as Madan Gokhle continued to chase his dream to be the chief minister after being cast into the role of a leader of opposition for a party that was set to come back with its divisive agenda. With elections around the corner, it was time for payback.

'I need you to understand that I'm not a turncoat politician. I've served the same party for 25 years. The world has to see what some people are about. Hatred breeds hatred.'

'Of course, I agree with you.'

'How soon could you write and publish my autobiography?' he looked at me with keen interest.

'I would say at least a year.'

'Do it in 8-9 months; the elections are around the corner. I'd like you to build it up and write the important chapters. I'll get some writers to fill up the more obvious information from my days as a minister.'

'Why me, and why us? You could go to someone bigger with this.'

'During my college days, I used to read books published by Kalim, and it would be a great honour if my book was published by you. Besides, there should be a surprise, shouldn't there? Otherwise, what's the fun? I don't want anyone to know I'm writing a book till it comes out.' *Crafty bugger!*

'Okay, I will get started right away.' *This is explosive!*

'Yes, go for it. Here's your advance. If there's anything else, do get in touch,' he said before getting up, signalling to me that the meeting was over. He walked away after exchanging formalities, and Jagan walked me back to the car. I opened the envelope and looked at my advance of ₹1.5 lakh and smiled to myself. It would pay off a third of my outstanding credit card debt in London. *Time to get to work.*

▪

I entered Gloria Jeans an hour later, where Anya Malik, looking prim and proper but definitely a more no-frills version of the images I had seen online, was sipping hot chocolate and reading *Vogue*. After an exchange of dry hellos, polite conversation about the weather and my unsuccessful writing career, we got down to business.

'So, I hear there's a new book in the offing. Tell me more,' I said with some interest.

She pulled out a bound script and handed it to me. 'What Will Become Of Us?' was the title in bold.

'It's a futuristic love story between two people who never meet. It's very tragic and slow but is a subject close to my heart.'

'I was hoping it would be something closer to what you've done before. But this is deep…and meaningful,' I added, seeing her set her gaze on me. She had sharp features and light green eyes like a Persian cat's.

'It is, and it's a departure from the pretentious bullshit I've written in the past. When I read it now, it makes me squirm.'

'Interesting…and has anyone else seen this book?'

'No, I've just mentioned it to my previous publisher, and he showed very little interest. He showed me the door, to be honest.'

'That's not a nice thing.'

'Oh, he's a sharp businessman.'

'What about the others?'

'I have no interest in dealing with them. If you don't do this one, I may just self-publish it or put it on a blog,' she said with some desperation in her voice.

'Okay, let me have a go at it. We'll have to see how to position this one, that's the challenge.'

'Oh you'll find a way, trust me,' she said with a warm smile and a glimmer in her eyes. *Is she flirting with me?*

'You shouldn't be so sure.'

'You're from Cambridge. I expect that you would as opposed to the rest. You wouldn't have these walls in your head.'

'I reckon it's reasonable to expect that.'

'My first novel was partly set in Cambridge, you know? The male protagonist is from there. It was my childhood dream to fall in love with this dashing, well-read and well-bred Englishman.' *She smiled at me invitingly and made me shift uncomfortably in my seat.*

'Is that so?' Zorah walked in just then with a curt smile, not looking very happy.

'Anya, this is Zorah. She's the marketing head of Kalim... and my girlfriend,' I added, which wiped that dreamy smile off her face. The girls barely smiled at each other. Anya looked nervous, and Zorah looked more hostile than she did with Sita.

'I should be running along. It's time for a family lunch and I shouldn't be late. I'll wait to hear from you, Akshay.'

'I'll get on it, and I'll be in touch,' I said, with Zorah's gaze fixed on me.

'Bye now,' Zorah said with her fake smile.

As soon as Anya left the café, there was a whack on my arm. 'Why were you flirting with her?'

'I wasn't! We were talking about her books and she asked me about Cambridge.' *Okay, there was some flirting.*

'You were clearly flirting. Smiling and giggling with her like a schoolboy. There's a glass window. I could see from outside.'

'Ah! Feeling jealous, are we?'

'No, what do I care? You can go out with her and discuss Keats and Wordsworth all your life.'

'Why would I do that? And you do feel insecure, although you say and pretend you don't.'

'Shut up! Let's go, isn't it time for the movie? I want to get popcorn before it starts.'

I walked out of the café with her arm in mine. My phone buzzed with a message. 'It was interesting meeting you, xx – Anya.' *Trouble.*

Day 97

$\mathcal{I}$ walked into office a few paces behind Zorah. We were still keeping it from Tarun and Sita that we were living together. Things were looking up, I was staying off the booze, spending a lot of time with Zorah, staying away from Anya Malik—who recently blogged her glowing review of my forgotten book—and I pushed ahead with Suryakant Joshi's story. Sensitive as it was, I was yet to break the whole thing to anyone at work, even Zorah.

'Oh Mr Akshay, there've been a lot of calls for you,' a harrowed-looking Sita said. *Did Roshan Khan plant some other story?* I was being invited to parties, baby showers and a dozen other celebrations, thanks to my association with him.

'Okay, send me a list of the messages you picked up.' I felt a tap on my shoulders and turned around to see an angry Tarun, standing a bit too close for comfort.

'What did you do, yaar?' *Well, if it isn't ol' grumpy with tummy trouble.*

'Good morning! What are you referring to?' I responded with a mean 'don't mess with me' look in my eyes.

'There was a story on *Breaking News* last night, and now this article in the paper.' He pushed it in my face and stood back with folded arms.

There was the usual rant about how I had gotten cozier with people in Bollywood, about my alleged girlfriend, Zorah, and me being seen often in the company of Roshan Khan and his hangers-on. Then it got serious; it went on about my preferences for celebrity writers and about me chasing publicity. *What the...* It continued with quotes from a dozen of the *Twilight* authors who felt let down about their book being binned. It had quotes like, 'He has no understanding or taste for Indian literature', 'He doesn't like us because we aren't good-looking, we don't drink wine or drive swanky cars' and 'He's only interested in the work of non-writers like Roshan Khan.' The 'he' here was yours truly, who, without having done anything, was paraded in the media as an asshole because he refused to flog a dead horse.

'How did it get so big? Why are they printing just my name? I thought we decided to not go ahead with *Twilight*.'

'That writer, Chitra Prakash, she's a former journalist. She's brought these people together and pulled some strings. Er... a few of them called me last week and I mentioned it was an editorial decision.' *Slippery son of a bitch.*

My phone buzzed; it was Angus, who had obviously received a copy of the article. 'Conference call now with you, Tarun and Zorah.'

What began as a shout and abuse as usual from him directed at the spineless Tarun and me was cleverly managed by Zorah, who cited that publicists were play here and that we needed to manage the situation carefully. I stood my ground and opposed publishing the book, knowing that it wouldn't work, but was pushed to the wall on this one by Angus and Tarun. So we agreed to do a small print run of the book and get it over with;

it would placate the authors and we could add it to the list as well. Tarun was asked to take charge and decide on that. Angus took a tough line on me, not taking kindly to the negative PR and the story of me romancing Iqbal Kalim's daughter.

'You've only signed two potentially good books, AK.'

'I'll get the others, Angus.'

'I'm increasingly worried. You've got like nine months, man.'

'I'm aware…'

'I think you should get on board a book or two, Tarun. AK doesn't have his head into mainstream Indian writing anyway. Go and pull out an author from one of the other publishers. I want three launches in the coming three months.'

'We've got *Twilight*, followed by Sudhir's debut novel, Roshan Khan's book is also coming up, Angus. It's difficult to line up a book so quickly. Editing takes time,' I reasoned.

'Maybe Tarun can find something that's ready to go to print. Let's leave to him, shall we?' he said curtly before hanging up. Tarun sat back with his smug grin.

'*Chalo*, I'll find something. We'll have to make it through this year, yaar.' He seemed pleased at undermining me, but the stress showed on his face. He was clearly unaware of what was going on. Literature and dealing with authors was a departure from category management of soaps, ice cream and energy drinks. I stepped out with Zorah for a smoke, and the nicotine, along with her cool reasoning, calmed me down.

'I think you should print 1,000 copies of *Twilight* and put them out there,' I said to Tarun on my way back to work.

'Leave it to me. I have a bigger idea—5,000 copies. We're getting a better deal with the printer, hardcover, with a launch in five cities. I'll work it all out. This will be big.' *No, it won't!*

A big hole in the pocket, if anything.

'I wouldn't do that, no.'

'Akshay, leave it to me. You worry about finding us books to publish.'

'Great! I would honestly print much less, but you call the shots here. I wish for us that you don't fuck this up.'

I went back to my office to see five missed calls on my phone. It was the sci-fi mad hatter, Sudhir. I called him back. 'I'm reaching your office in 10 minutes. We have to talk,' he said, before hanging up.

Ten minutes later, he walked in, looking noticeably irritated.

'What bit you?'

'Saw this story of yours in the paper. You're dating Zorah? And you're running around with this Roshan Khan?' *Oh that's what! Especially, the first part. So, what you're going to do?*

'I don't believe I need to answer questions about my life and what I do with my time.'

'Boss, this isn't done, huh! You make me do so much editing; my book looks far from being published and you're running around with your marketing girl and that superficial steroid junkie. You have no time for authors like me…'

'Your book needs work. You need to put in effort on my comments. We're trying to take your book to the next level…'

'I want my book published, boss. Two months, else I take it to one of the bigger guys.'

'We are ready when you are.' This guy really made me regret the day I agreed to publish his book.

'You people ignore me and hang out with this actor and his friends.'

'No one's ignoring you, man. Let's go and have lunch.

Zorah, you and I. Do you want to go to Roshan Khan's party this weekend?'

'Really?' He tapped the table and shook my hand vigorously. 'Yeah, sure.' *Oh hell!*

Day 100

$\mathcal{S}$uddenly, office was abuzz with activity. Even poor old Mr Samuel was working the phone with his distributors and the printer. Tarun was gung-ho. It was the first opportunity to prove himself and he'd already put his grubby fingers into our tiny marketing budget and pulled 15 per cent out of it for the launch of *Twilight*. Posters and bookmarks were commissioned and events were lined up at leading bookstores across the country. Authors of this great book had gone from being upset to sending friendly overtures, with messages asking about a sequel and whether they could send in more stories for the same. The newly-launched website featured all of them, along with the likes of Sudhir, Roshan Khan and Vinod Dutta as 'Our Authors'. Zorah was putting in phenomenal effort on publicity and had lined up a spate of interviews with newspapers and TV channels for some of the authors and myself, given I was named along with the late Iqbal Kalim as the editor of the collection. Zorah walked in looking excited.

'I've lined up a television interview for you.'

'Okay, I could do that. What language do I have to talk in?'

'Don't be funny. Gaurav Bedi, the famous book critic, who

anchors the biggest TV show on books, wants to chat with you. He's getting here in an hour with his cameraman.'

'What? Here in our office?'

'Yeah, he wanted to come in here. He says the place has historical significance; he's very old-school and a queer sort. My dad and he were friends, and then had a falling out of sorts. I guess he's doing it to show his respect or something.'

'Sounds interesting!' *Old Kalim knew an interesting set of people.*

A little over an hour later, an old gentleman with a handlebar moustache and wearing a grey suit walked into my office with a glum cameraman and a nervous Zorah, who stood a few steps away with an awkward look, and an eager-to-please Tarun.

After brief exchanges on where I came from and what I had done, the conversation launched into back-and-forth questions on what we were publishing, my plans for the firm and the like. I kept it calm and balanced, and revealed little about Vinod Dutta's book or about plans to sign on Anya Malik or any other specific project at the back of my mind. The old man took a few digs at my Bollywood lifestyle, and I let him have it, adding, much to his delight, 'I love India and our people. I love this firm and my job. I don't see myself going back. I see myself back home, here in Mumbai.' With that, we wrapped up for the evening and I saw the proud smile on Zorah's face that shone like the stars one can see in the countryside on a clear night.

'I had a favour to ask of you,' Bedi said, before he left the cabin.

'Sure, anything.'

'I have this book, a memoir of sorts. I've written about my travels, the books I've enjoyed and about some of the interesting people I've met.' *Ah! There's the hook.*

'Sounds interesting.'

'Maybe I could send it to you. I really want to get it published. I've been working on it for years.'

'Sure, please do.'

He walked out with a broad smile, not before patting my back and calling me the future of Indian publishing. I went back to editing Sudhir's masterpiece and had a conference call with the authors of *Bottled Up*, discussing the essays about the depressing state of the nation. I initially thought that they might be suicidal after writing such a book but they seemed very confident and attached to what they'd written, and eagerly wanted to see this get published to create awareness among the youth. Anya sent me constant reminders regarding feedback on her futuristic love story. She sent me a folder of pictures from her personal photoshoot that could be used in the publicity of the book. The book in itself was a confused potboiler, something that needed a lot of work by a capable editor, almost a complete rewrite, to salvage Anya's efforts on the title.

I had to fend off her requests to meet for lunch or a drink, and those quotes that ended with '☺'. Roshan decided to play friend and gave me a call as well.

'Man, you've been getting some heat from the press these days. I just heard that the *Hindustan Times* newspaper is printing your picture with a caption, "Bollywood Ass-kisser".'

'Come on Khan, you can take care of it, man. Ask them not to do this!'

'Ha ha…I was messing with you, buddy.'

'Ah, alright.'

'Actually, I had half a mind to do it. It would be funny. Ha ha.'

'Ha ha! Come on, man!' *Choke, groan.*

'Yeah, I'll see you at my party tonight. Let's smoke some weed and be merry. Are you bringing the girlfriend?'

'Yes, I'll be there with Zorah, and another friend, Sudhir.'

'Alright! Didn't know you were swinging?' *I can't explain what my life has become.*

'No, man, nothing like that.'

'No, don't worry; it's a free world; we're cool, man. See you tonight.'

There was a tap on my door. Sita stood ahead of a guy who looked like he was interviewing for a tea boy's job.

'Mr Akshay, this man insists that he has to meet you. He says he's a writer and that you've been in touch.' The lad stood behind her with a goofy smile and waved at me.

'Let him in, Sita,' I said, to which she moved aside and walked away in a huff.

'Thank you, sir. I'm Mihin Shah, I just come from Madurai on work.' *Damn!*

'What can I do for you?'

'How are you, sir? I see Zorah *bhabi* and your pictures in the paper. When is the wedding?' he asked with his toothy grin.

'Who are you, again? Can we talk about why you're in my office?'

'Yes, you rejected my book, na! It's very good, yaar. You should publish it. Only Roshan Khan isn't talented.' *Oh come on! Not again.*

'I think we've given you a decision. Best of luck on your next novel, and I hope this one finds a worthy publisher.' *1,2,3…*

He stood up and banged his fist on my table. 'You no like ordinary man. I leave job to write my book and you reject it…

What you think? That Roshan Khan is a crazy fellow. I warn you,' he screamed, before rushing out of my office. *What the fuck was that?*

A moment later, Zorah, followed by the others, came into my office. 'Don't worry, he's some guy whose work we turned down. We should talk to the security about letting these guys in.'

After contemplating the manic episode for a while, I decided not to tell Roshan Khan anything, lest it become another attempt at PR and something to laugh at with his cronies. I called Jagan instead, who sounded furious.

'How dare he talk to you like that? Don't worry, Akshay Sahib. I will break his hands and legs. He will not come near you or anyone in Kalim Publishing.'

'No Jagan, please don't hit him. A warning will do.' *After all, I'm not some mafia just a celebrity ass-kisser.*

'*Haan haan*,' I'll settle that fellow. Don't worry, sir. I'll keep the phone now.'

I hung up and went out for a smoke with Zorah, feeling bad about the entire incident. These poor guys were driven by what they saw around them. They wanted to get to where someone else was, never mind if they lacked the talent. We ended up laughing about the incident by the end of it and got back to work.

Tarun came in looking excited an hour later. 'You've got to listen to this. An author who is with Hatcher Rollins, Asmita Seth, wants to give us rights to her book *Stems and Petals*.'

'A book that's already published?'

'Yes, four months ago. She's really unhappy with the editors. The publisher didn't market her book well and the paper quality of the book is cheaper than what it normally uses.'

'What do you want to do?'

'We need books, Akshay! Remember what Angus said. I'm signing her on, yaar. I need more books. We need to survive. We can re-launch this after *Twilight*.'

'It would be good if I read the book and the reviews…'

'I've decided, yaar, we're going ahead on this one. Asmita Seth lives in my brother's building; she's well connected and influential too. She works at United Indian Bank.' *Go figure, how does this even matter?*

'Okay, well this is your call. I don't recommend taking on books before reading them, but I hope it works for the firm.' *Shoot me.*

'It will, I tell you this will work. I will begin plans on launch and promotion.' I needed to go out for another smoke. To add to it all, I had to show up in character as Roshan Khan's bitch tonight.

Day 108

'AK, wake up! Take your bloody phone yeah…it's ringing so early in the morning.'

'Let me sleep, Zo. Ten minutes, please.' I turned away and buried my head under the pillow. We had had a very late night at Roshan Khan's son's birthday party.

'Someone's trying to reach you. You may as well see who it is.'

'Why don't you see? Take it for me, please.'

'I'm not taking Tarun's or Sudhir's call, huh!' *Screw them, don't take their call at all.*

'It's *that* Anya Malik,' she said, shaking me.

'Who?' *Oh man.*

'You heard me!'

I sat up and took my mobile phone from her, before she went to bury her head under the pillow.

'Yeah?'

'AK, how are you? Did I wake you up? Saw your picture in the paper, such a nice article. You know, I haven't heard from you. I wanted to meet you to discuss my book. I had an idea…'

'Come over to my office at 4 p.m.' *Please wear something that covers your cleavage.*

'Thanks, AK! Byeeee,' she said, before blowing kisses on the phone and hanging up. *Phew!*

'It's just about that book of hers,' I said, looking at Zorah, who continued to stay in bed.

'Whatever,' she hissed. *Here we go again. I'm back in the doghouse.*

'Let's lie down for a bit,' I said, as I snuggled closer to her.

'No! Go for your shower,' she said, treating me like a repulsive rat.

'Let's both go for a shower.'

'I said no. I'm not in the mood,' she said, pushing me away. An hour later, we were at work, and I set my eyes on the newspaper that Tarun had brought to my office.

'Wonderful, yaar!' he said, before throwing it before me and walking away.

There was a half-page article about me with a nice Photoshop touched-up image. 'Dickens of the East', the title said. It spoke favourably about my growing-up years, how I had been discovered as a promising writer while at Cambridge, my 'success' as a writer and an editor of a magazine in London with blurbs from favourable reviews, a kind word from a British writer and more glowing praises from writers and journalists in India, including one from the *Twilight* family. It closed with a quote ostensibly made by me, 'I'm here with the dream of taking English language and literature to the common man, and particularly to the poor. I won't rest till it's done. I pledge to donate half of my earnings towards this cause.' *That's so cheesy. When the hell did I say this? I haven't even been drinking. Freakin' Roshan Khan, bastard!*

A rival tabloid, however, decided that this was something

they could have fun with. NGOs, teachers, old aunties with no better work and some other odd characters in need of PR praised my views and dreams, hoping that there were more like me, and that this was the need of the hour. Suryakant Joshi opined, 'Akshay is right, education is the need of the hour.' Roshan Khan called me 'the new king of English literature in India' and added that 'AK is here to conquer'. Gaurav Bedi called me 'the pioneer of a new revolution and a voice that couldn't be ignored'. *Thank you, that should find me new enemies.* Anya Malik cooed, 'He's the sexiest Indian editor around. Everyone else is fat, old or ugly.' *Some more enemies!*

The owner of JR Books, Jaidev Roy, launched into an attack mode, saying, 'Why should education be only in English? He has no respect for our *bhasha*.' A spokesperson for the Apna Democratic Party described Roshan Khan and me as ISI agents and demanded that we move to Pakistan. The spokesperson from the Leftists quoted Mao and called me 'a slave to the Queen and the Pope'. He felt it important to add that 'India isn't ruled by the British any more' and that I should close my 'East India Company and go back'. Another author, whom we had incidentally rejected and whose book recently made it to the bestseller list, said, 'Akshay is a dopehead who parties with Roshan Khan. He has no understanding of India. His India is Pali Hill. He keeps talking about poor people to show a poor image of India to the West. The truth is India is shining and we are the new superpower.' *Oh go to hell, man! How did you even manage a sentence without typos? It must've needed heavy-duty ghostwriting from the editors.*

Zorah lightened up on reading the tabloid piece that also showed me dancing with a drunk Roshan Khan. She was in splits reading the quotes and, at the end of it, there were tears in her eyes.

'I didn't say any of those things. I haven't even met this journalist! When did she interview me?'

'I know she didn't. It must be Roshan Khan trying to give you and himself some PR.' My life had become a circus, and I loathed this kind of unwanted attention.

I received an SMS from Gaurav Bedi just then. 'Congrats on the great coverage! The editor of the paper is a great friend. We felt the coverage could give you some character, you know. Bring you on our side, the side of respectable English literature. Hope you're enjoying my memoir.' *The bloody old fox!*

'It was Gaurav Bedi, the old coot. He has no better work.'

'Yeah, you better be careful. He's trying to draw you into his little incestuous circle.'

'Oh, this is crazy!' I got another text. It was from a Sonia Seth: 'Hi, please come for the opening of my art gallery in Khar with Zorah. I will text you the time and address. It would be lovely to have you. Gaurav is an old friend and speaks highly of you. It would be good to finally meet you.'

I showed Zorah the message and she was in splits again. 'You're really making it big on the Page 3 circuit.' *Yeah, from partying with junkies to sipping wine with snooty arty types. Quite a fucking journey!*

'Let's just go for a smoke,' I said, after replying "thank you" to Gaurav Bedi and "yes, for sure" to Soniya Seth, whom I'd never met in my life.

Roshan Khan stormed into office after lunch with a photographer, his man Friday and a secretary lurking around.

'Hey, AK! Wild party last night, huh?'

'Yeah, sure was. Why did you take the trouble to come? You should have called.'

'Yeah, buddy! See, I want to do something big with the book. I want to plan a big launch. Something like what we do to launch a film or a music release. It has to have glitz and glamour. I'm getting an event management company to work with the bookstores.' *Why, God why?*

'We really...'

'I'll have them put up laminated posters of me across all bookstores. Just like you see outside cinemas, na. We can also take up window displays for the book at these stores. It's my book and it has to be big. I've already worked out with newspaper editors to carry a one-page excerpt from the book.'

'Okay, let's do all of that.' *Now get out of here. Leave me in peace.*

'You have had nice publicity today, huh? You like what I said, na?'

'Thanks, Khan! You're the man.' *That's not me; I didn't say that.*

'No problem, buddy! It was funny what that old communist said: "Slave to the Queen and the Pope." Ha ha!'

'Ha ha.' *Fucking hilarious, isn't it? Ironically, it is.*

'Buddy, I have a surprise for you.' *Groan! I don't want another PlayStation.*

'Hit me.' *Yeah really! Go for it.*

'There's a party at my place this Saturday. Zorah and you are the hosts. It's a theme party. Everyone has to show up in a costume from the Victorian times. Invites have gone out and the designers are working in full swing. I've asked them to make something for both of you. I've arranged some A-grade stash too.'

'Oh man, the press will have a field day. I have these Leftists and hardliners baying for my blood.'

'Ha ha, don't worry! It'll be a lot of fun. You're the "Dickens of the East" anyway.'

'I'll tell Zorah about it, thanks.'

'No problem. I've asked my guys to invite all your friends. All those people who said nice things about you in the papers are invited. And some who didn't,' he snorted with a wink. *Damn! Anya Malik is coming*!

'You didn't have to, man!'

'What are friends for! Now, here's the thing. I'm not completely happy with the book. A journalist friend says it's too dry and too clean. It needs to be more fun and peppier. There has to be some mischief in it that goes with my personality,' he said, propping himself up with an air of superiority.

'Yeah, I guess. It needs to be livened up a bit.'

'Do you know what I want? Give it some life. Add bits of fun here and there. You know me and the gang.'

'Yeah, I'll do it.' *I'll make it so funny that you're going to cry.*

'Great, buddy! So, do you want to invite this ass-wipe, Tarun, to the party?'

'We aren't having ghazals for music or that *bhang,* are we?' *Also, bar dancers who'd go home with the likes of him.*

'No, yeah, I guess he's very downmarket for a party like this. Let him read about it in the papers.'

Roshan Khan's departure brought the arrival of Anya Malik into my office. I requested Zorah to join us as well.

Anya wore a low-cut floral dress with an ample display of her cleavage and her shapely bosom. 'Thanks for the invite again! I'm so excited.'

'Sure, look forward to seeing you there,' I said, watching Zorah walk in with a frown.

'Let's do this quickly, as we have a couple of other meetings,' Zorah said with some contempt.

'Yes, it's a very interesting book, but I worry,' I added. *You're a tad more interesting. Shut up dude, Zorah will kill you.*

'Uh-huh! Go on,' she smiled seductively, gazing at me intently. *Oh boy, she's something. But Zorah's something else. Focus!*

'I think it doesn't go with your image, and your readers expect something lighter from you.' *Maybe something where they'd have to leave their brains at home.*

'But the gravity of emotion here is very real; I believe in these things,' she said looking hurt.

'I know that, but this isn't what your perceived image is. This can damage the book's potential.'

'Well then, what do you want me to do? It's been almost two years since my last release. Readers will forget about me if I don't come out with something,' she said, looking from Zorah to me, and flashing me her sultry smile.

'We'll discuss and think about it,' Zorah said, to which I added, 'There may be a solution. See you at the party.'

Anya smiled, Zorah frowned, and I went back to the doghouse.

Day 120

$\mathcal{Z}$orah walked into my cabin almost in tears, while I was absorbed in editing a paragraph I'd written for Suryakant Joshi's book. She collapsed on the seat opposite me, and expected me to sit up and listen.

'What is Tarun troubling you about?' Tarun had been on her case about the launch of *Twilight*, interfering in every little detail and adding his cheap sensibilities to the things that Zorah was planning. He wanted this book to be his quick win. He wanted to show Angus Lee that here was a man who could sell books.

'It's not him, really! It is him to an extent, but this Sudhir is chewing my brains.'

'What's his problem?'

'He's pestering me to try and set up a launch for him at the big, independent stores in London and New York.' *Wannabe son of a bitch!*

'Oh, that jobless hack! Tell him that they don't have a clue about him. They wouldn't just host a launch for him and his book.'

'Exactly! They are asking who the hell is this guy. And he refuses to listen or reason. He just wants it done. He wants posters of the book in the London Underground stations. He wants it up on all kinds of lists.'

'Calm down. Just say yes and that you're trying your best.'

'He keeps sending me these "status update ASAP" messages.'

'I'll talk this out with him.' *Maybe I'll just shoot the arrogant bastard.*

'It's really challenging to work with this moron, AK,' she said, making a small face.

'Hmm ... let me deal with him. Let me take you out for lunch.'

My phone buzzed with Sudhir's call at the same time. I cut his call and sent him a text. 'In a meeting, can't do this now. Please get to our office at 5. We need to talk.'

Three hours later, he strode in; his hair was a mess and he hadn't shaved for days. I sent Zorah away to meet our publicists on some pretext.

He looked upset and aloof. 'Boss, this is unprofessional, huh! Zorah is *not* the most cooperative person to work with. She needs to show more passion.'

'Actually, coming to that, we need to discuss your book. It's taking way too much time and effort. The management wants us to defer the release or drop it.'

'What?' *Gotcha!*

'Yeah, you know Zorah and I are spending half our time on this. The leadership asks whether we work for the company or for you?'

'I'm just working towards a great and successful launch.'

'I understand.' *Yeah right, you greedy bastard!*

'I can't do it without your support...' *I know that too.*

'Unfortunately, I think we'll need to end this one. I was

trying to get Roshan to launch your book in Mumbai and an interview with Gaurav Bedi. But...'

'What do you want me to do? I want to make this work...' he moaned.

'Well, let's see. You need to find someone to copy edit and proofread your work. We need to receive a manuscript that is reasonably well edited, not work-in-progress like we have here... We can't afford to go back and forth on Twitter.'

'Will be done.' *That was easy.*

'You need to get a full-time publicist to organize whatever you need. We'll just help with Mumbai and sending this book for reviews.'

'Yes, I could have someone do that.' *Poor someone, but good for us!*

'Good, I look forward to making this a success, then.'

His face lit up and he seemed relieved as he sat back into the chair.

'So, are you coming for the party this weekend?'

'Oh yes! I got the invitation.'

'Yeah, it was one of the first I sent out.'

'It had Zorah's name also on it.'

'Yeah, we're hosting it together.' *So? Do the math, asshole!*

'She is your serious girlfriend or what?'

'Yeah, we've been seeing each other.'

'Shit, man! Very good, she's hot!'

'Yeah, I got lucky. Else she would have gone for you.' *More like gone through you with a knife.*

'I know, that's right, man. We would have made a good couple. But good for you, man.'

'So what are you coming dressed as?'

'What do you suggest? I'm not really familiar with all this Victorian-times nonsense.'

'You should come dressed as Fagin from *Oliver Twist*. He was a much-loved character among the young.' *Ha ha, yeah right!*

'Good, I'll do something like that.'

'Yeah! Get a costume and some make-up. The press will be there.'

'Good idea.'

'I'll have you meet Anya Malik. She's a popular writer, and a very attractive girl. She'll be at the party too. You can Google her.'

'Good, man! I'll come dressed like that Fagin. And I can't wait to meet this hot writer chick.'

'Yeah, good to see you! And look, Zorah and I are hands off on your book from now. You work with your people and work through Sita. Get in touch with her if you want to set up meetings. We've got to really manage time on this one.'

'I understand,' he said, gritting his teeth.

'See you at the party.'

'Yeah, man! Say hello to Zorah for me.'

'Sure, bye now.'

I had just gone back to Joshi's novel when I got a call from a journalist asking about Vinod Dutta's novel.

'What do you want to know? It's a little early to talk about it.'

'He mentions that you'll be publishing his most special piece of work.'

'That's right!'

'He's been in and out of the hospital lately.'

'I know, that's really sad. We want him to recover before the launch.'

'It doesn't seem like he'll last long. His organs are failing.'

'It's a shame,' I sighed.

'Can you tell us what is this about?'

'All I can say is that it is revolutionary. It's the Vinod Dutta you haven't seen before. You'll be very surprised.' *Very surprised.*

'How interesting! I will quote you on that,' she said, before hanging up.

I sat back and wondered about his book, thinking about the best way to play it forward. A germ of an idea entered my mind that made me grin like a tropical monkey. *You bad boy, you!*

Day 135

$\mathcal{Z}$orah and I lurked around at the back of the bookstore, watching the proceedings with some embarrassment as Tarun progressively lost his cool with authors, the staff at the store and the photographer, who, for some reason, kept clicking his picture. A small group of nine people showed up for the launch, many of whom were relatives and friends of the authors. A newbie journalist from a languishing daily showed up, took bytes from the authors, along with a free copy of the book, and left hastily before the book discussion began. The store manager, an old hand, stood in the background and grinned at the hapless Tarun, who held the store responsible for the poor turnout to launch his epic. The store was plastered with posters that he'd gotten laminated and copies were stacked at various places in the store.

'I'm sure it will pick up by word of mouth,' I said, trying to placate Tarun.

'No, these guys have failed to bring in a crowd, yaar! Why is the media not here, Zorah?' he growled.

'Invites were sent to everyone, Tarun. There's the premiere of a much-awaited film today. Most of the media is covering that event. We will, however, send them pictures,' she said calmly.

'I think the store manager wants to have a word with you,' I said, breaking up the conversation. I led Zorah outside and stepped away for a smoke. The launch was a disaster and neither of us could salvage that. *Hopefully, he'll realize that he bet on the wrong horse.*

'It's bad for us, huh? We've launched with a book like this,' a worried Zorah said between long drags.

'Who is going to tell him? He keeps at it with his "I'm the boss" routine. He's got to realize that he cannot take creative decisions.'

'We should have begun with Roshan Khan's book.'

'I know, but he's got that banker's book next. He seems very gung-ho about re-launching that one. And then we have good old Sudhir, whom I most certainly want to be done with.'

'Let's hope that works,' she said, as we walked back to the bookstore.

'Well, I'm not too optimistic,' I said. 'I apologize for sounding cynical, but I hope I'm proved wrong.' The staff had started piling up the chairs in one corner, shelves were being dragged back to their places and glum-faced authors were walking towards the exit.

Three days later, the mood in the office was still tense. The next release was held in Bengaluru, which was a washout due to sudden rain. The evening after that was the launch in Delhi that Tarun had flown down for, which had no media presence, one of the authors failed to show up predicting that it would be a debacle, and there were five people in the audience. A livid Tarun nearly went to blows with the store manager, who ignored his questions on the audience turnout. He moped around in office, barking orders at Zorah, Sita and even Mr Samuel, who was working the phone all day to persuade stores to place orders. I stayed away from the action, locked in my cabin and adding dashes of masala to my friend, Roshan Khan's novel.

Zorah entered, looking harrowed. 'Just got a call from a journalist friend. Vinod Dutta was reportedly hospitalized last night. He's gone into a coma.'

'Hmm...let's go down there and pay him a visit tonight.'

'What do you plan to do with his book?'

'I think it's time to launch it. Maybe soon after Roshan Khan's book would be a good idea.'

Tarun stormed in to take Zorah away from my office. He had increasingly begun to look at us with disdain, and the feelings were mutual. He'd stopped talking to me beyond the bare minimum about work since he had seen pictures from the party that Zorah and I had hosted at Roshan Khan's place, which was attended by Anya, Sudhir and many others who smiled for the shutterbugs. Angus was told of the office romance but he refused to have anything to say or do about it, leaving it to adults to make their own choices. This angered Tarun even more, and I had heard him tell Sita how it was unprofessional for Zorah and me to step out for a smoke. I could hear them arguing outside, with Zorah telling him that despite her efforts, two mentions and a thumbnail picture in a tabloid was the best coverage she could manage for the launch. After coercing her to push more and try harder, he rushed back to his cabin to work the phone himself.

Post-lunch, Sudhir, showing that old habits die hard, strode in with a worried look on his face.

'I don't think we had a meeting planned, did we?'

'Boss, it's important. I have to talk to you,' he said, with an urgency in his voice.

'Okay, I'm really busy, but go ahead.'

'I don't know what you guys are up to, boss! There's nothing in the papers about your book *Twilight*'s launch. There's no buzz about it, nobody is talking about the book. Most people don't know a thing about it and those who do say it's a flop.'

'You're telling me something that I already know.'

'I'm very worried. I'm throwing everything behind my book and depending on you guys.'

'We asked you to get a publicist, right?'

'Yes, but you guys…'

'You do that, and don't worry about books like *Twilight*. It was accepted for publishing a year back, even before any of us joined. We had to do it to fulfill old commitments.'

'I read the book, boss, and it's quite boring.' *And yours is a page-turner!*

'I'm aware, Sudhir. Can you focus on your book? The launch is two months away; we can focus on it closer to the date, yeah?'

'Okay, if you can assure me that we won't have a *Twilight*-like disaster.'

'I think your book has way more potential, Sudhir. Believe in your talent, and find a publicist,' I said, trying to sound as convincing as possible, although deep in my heart I knew that this was a mistake I'd made under pressure.

'Yeah, that's great! I think it can be the #1 bestseller.'

'Yes, let's work towards that.' *If it goes past its first print run, it'll be a relief.*

'Boss, can you give me Anya Malik's number. We were hanging out at your party and I forgot to save her number.' *Nice try. I saw her ignore your pitiable advances.*

'Sorry, I can't do that, man. But try connecting on Facebook and Twitter.'

'I don't think she's that active, boss. I left her a few messages.'

'That's a shame. I'll let her know when I see her. Have a good day, man. Work on the editing,' I said with a straight face, shaking his hand and leading him out of my cabin. He stood there for a moment, looking at Tarun blow his lid with someone over the phone. An hour later, a sombre Mr Samuel told me that returns had begun pouring in from retailers who had no faith in *Twilight*.

'I can't remember seeing copies returned at such a furious pace when Iqbal was around,' he said, shaking his head.

I dug into myself and kept working on Roshan's and Suryakant Joshi's books. An hour before leaving for the hospital to see Vinod Dutta, Zorah and I had an intense brainstorming discussion on the marketing of the books I was betting on.

Day 144

The few reviews that appeared of *Twilight* were disappointing, to say in the least. The best thing that was said about the book was that it was painfully well edited. The most common feedback was that the stories didn't come together as a single collection and that the book probably released 10 years too late. The audience's tastes had evolved and the current generation had no appetite for books about opulent lives of long-forgotten royals in old havelis, a hidden gulley in Kolkata or a decaying peepul tree somewhere. Tarun moped about in a blue funk and blamed bookstores, authors and even Iqbal Kalim for coming up with a 'foolish' compilation. He appeared confident about the re-launch of *Stems and Petals* and worked zealously to repeat everything he had done for *Twilight*. I overheard him talking to distributors about a 'buy two and take one copy of *Twilight*' scheme.

Meanwhile, I received a call from Gaurav Bedi, who requested me to meet him for cocktails at Four Seasons. I had just finished reading his laborious memoir and decided to turn it down, given its very limited appeal in the Indian market. *I'll let the old man know once he's down a few drinks. Maybe I could use Tarun's name.*

Before I could slip away with Zorah for lunch, Roshan Khan strode into my office with his usual entourage. He sported a day-old stubble, and wore dark glares and Bermuda shorts.

'AK! I wanted to run some of the plans for the launch past you, buddy.'

'Yeah sure.'

'There's a lot of buzz about my book. Everyone's anticipating the release of my story. How many method actors exist in Bollywood? Not many, just me in the top bracket.' *Talk about self–delusion.*

'Why don't I change the name of one chapter to "The Method Man"?'

'Good idea!'

'This book will see you in a new light, Khan.' *Ugh.*

'Yes, I'm negotiating two big international films on the back of the hype of this book. Things are looking up.'

'That's great!'

'Now I'm going to be on all major news channels to talk about the book. I'm also shooting a 10-minute DVD on the making of the book, with interviews from people I've done favours to in the industry. I want a byte or two from you as well.'

'Yes, sure.' *Can I be honest? No? Damn!*

'Come down now. I've brought my Honda X500 for you to ride. I'll ride my Hayabusa. Let's zip around town on the bikes for a bit.' *What are we? 16?*

'I kind of have meetings in some time.'

'Oh, fuck that! Come on, buddy. Let it go for half an hour. My photographer is here too. We'll feed it to the papers this week.' *The things a man has to do for his livelihood!*

'Well, okay, we could do a short ride.'

'Yes, that's the spirit! Now what are the plans this weekend?'

'Nothing yet. Zorah and I plan to take it ...' *Don't tell me of another lame excuse to party!*

'Great! I have tickets for you and Sameer to go and watch the Arsenal vs Chelsea game. First-class tickets on Virgin Atlantic to London.'

'I'm a Manchester United fan. But why me? I'm not sure...' I managed, trying not to sound furious on being treated as his son's babysitter.

'Well, see, the wife is going away on a hush-hush girl's trip. They're hitting some spas and letting their hair down a bit. I'm shooting for a commercial with this young bombshell from the South in Goa. I could use some alone time with her. And what Manchester? You're from London, na? Go enjoy the game. Sameer really wants to see Arsenal win.' *So, I guess that makes me an Arsenal supporter.*

'Well, alright.' *I'm going to get you for this.*

'Let's go. Hope the changes to the book are going well.' *You mean your narcissist propaganda.*

'Yes, I'm spicing it up.'

'Great, buddy! You're getting a hang of the celeb life by being with me.'

I was back an hour later, sweating like a pig, having ridden a sports bike wearing formal trousers, a shirt and a tie. Zorah giggled when she saw me enter with my hair spiked up and Tarun turned away looking like he'd seen a mad man. Anya Malik walked in a short while later and cooed about how dashing I looked riding around near her apartment on a sports bike.

'I love fast bikes but the problem is that they're gas-guzzlers.

Therefore, I'll never sit on one,' she gushed. *I wasn't going to ask you to.*

'Yeah, sure they are.' *You herbal-tea-loving, tree-hugging freak!*

'I had a lot of fun at the party the other day. The only irritant was that guy dressed like some old man from the Victorian Age who kept bragging about some sci-fi adventure novel. Freak!'

'Sudhir, you mean?'

'Yes, he's been sending me these incessant emails about catching up to discuss books and the like.' *Yeah, you should hook up with him.*

'Yeah, he's quite the passionate one.' *More like the cheap and obsessive type.*

'Totally not my type! I think charm is reflected in the way one carries oneself,' she said, smiling at me suggestively and pouting her lips. *Here we go again.*

'Anyway, let's discuss your book.'

'I'm open to any ideas you might have. I just want to see this getting published...'

'See, the deal is that I can't go ahead with your submission.' Her expression changed from a flirty smile to one of deep embarrassment. 'I have to be honest—it's not worth sticking your name out on this one.'

'What am I going to do? Even my last book...'

'I might have a plan,' I said, before I got up and shut the door, as I didn't want Sita or Tarun to listen in.

Late that evening, pleased with the turn of events with Anya, who was excited with my plan, I managed to get Gaurav Bedi drunk beyond his usual limits, although I got a bit wasted as well. I had to sit through stories of people in journalism and publishing I didn't know, scandalous revelations about the skeletons in their closet, their preferences and their libidos, and Bedi's resentment for a couple of big-shot editors as they had refused to publish his memoir.

'I can bring you a dozen good books that my friends have written and these fools have turned down,' he said in his drunken stupor. *By friends, you mean other snooty old cracks like you?*

'I'm quite certain they've passed up some good work. There's a lot of talent.'

'Bah, it's filled with this lazy, full-of-themselves lot. All they do is organize wine and cheese soirées in Delhi and make themselves heard at literature festivals. They are destroying Indian literature.' *A case of pot calling the kettle black!*

'Er…yes, about your book, I'm afraid we cannot move ahead on this one. Tarun is opposed to it. He says it's not marketable enough.'

'What! Oh, that bloody uncouth fellow! He used to sell candy bars, right?' he demanded furiously.

'Ice cream, actually, and then energy drinks. He was the sales head of a division of a company that did.'

'Oh, it's horrible, you know. These fools running around thinking that they know what good literature is. Does he think *Twilight* is a great book? Does that buffoon even read?'

'What to do? My wings are clipped and my hands are tied. He wants only young writers, preferably young, pretty women.' *I think I'm talking too much.*

'Oh, I'm very disappointed, you know. Yet, these vulgar Bollywood fellows have no trouble finding publishers. Bastards! It's become so crass and commercial, it's depressing,' he said, before sipping angrily from his glass of scotch.

Half an hour later, I had to help him get to his car and have his driver take care of him, but not before he abused the owner of his TV station, other editors in the business, Tarun and even Roshan Khan. Zorah called as I was leaving the hotel.

'Are you drunk with your old friend or do you have room for some more. There's a bottle of wine I wanted to open...in the bathtub,' she said in a saucy voice.

'I'll be there in 15 minutes.' *Perfect stress buster*!

'Hurry,' she said with a laugh before hanging up.

Day 151

$\mathcal{I}$ heard nothing from Gaurav Bedi after our evening at Four Seasons. *Stems and Petals* had been launched a week back to a lukewarm reception from the audience. The author, Riya Oberoi, did manage to bring in a crowd of people who supported and cheered her on but there was little interest in the media about the lives and frustrations of middle-aged women who lived in high-rises, woke up at 11 a.m. and preoccupied themselves with shopping for designer wear, undergoing makeovers and showing up at parties. I guess people had their fill with daily soap operas and, considering their own mundane existence, looked for escapism or intellectual stimulation to modern literature. At the very least, the audience was looking for subjects that dealt with affairs of the heart and angst among the youth. This book offered neither of those and was a dull, depressing story that portrayed a very pessimistic view of life. The morning's paper had had a scathing review of the book by guest reviewer Gaurav Bedi. He also managed to pull his punches at Tarun, who was described as a 'misfit for a literary publishing house with a great heritage', and me for 'being distracted and swayed by glamour and cheap publicity in Bollywood'. He claimed that writers and book lovers were 'disappointed, as Akshay Mathur had great potential to make a difference. But it appears he is an editor with a price tag and neither has the power nor the inclination to do so. Akshay remains a puppet in Kalim's dog and pony show in the name of publishing.'

Tarun was livid as usual and had to be stopped from calling Gaurav Bedi and giving him an earful of the choicest Hindi expletives. He ranted about suing the newspaper and got into a fight on the phone with a senior journalist. I was quite taken aback myself and was surprised by his bitter attack. The next day saw three other reviews flowing in, one on *Twilight*, which trashed the book and called it 'garbage', and two on *Stems and Petals*, which said 'read it if you want to kill yourself' and 'depressing, convoluted and unconvincing plot'. Tarun flew into fits of rage and had to be told to calm down so that he could think clearly. Sudhir, Anya, Roshan and the other authors were upset by the sharp criticism of our efforts. Zorah managed to set up a television interview for Roshan and me with Sohail Malik, a witty anchor on Now TV and who had quite a disdain for Gaurav Bedi.

Roshan walked in prepared to milk this opportunity to the best of his advantage. He was inclined to play it to the gallery and generate maximum interest for his book. We walked in on the sets of the chat show to the applause of a cheering crowd. After a warm welcome and an exchange of pleasantries, Sohail began to needle him.

'You haven't had much success with your recent films, now suddenly there's this book. Why?' *It's obvious that he has little to do!*

'Well, Sohail, you never know with films, though I have

loved each one that I've been part of. But the audience likes some of them, and some don't work for various reasons. One has to respect the audience and their verdict. My book is a gift to my fans and everyone who has supported me. I came, I saw, I conquered—and this is who I am,' he said with a confident smile. *Not a bad actor!*

'So is it another tell-all account? Because that's what seems to be in vogue.'

'It is an honest look at my life and my time in the industry. It's dedicated to everyone who's been part of that journey.'

'Why now?' *He's desperate for some publicity. Throwing parties every week only gets you so far!*

'I took this decision to really look hard and pick the right subjects. While I've been doing that, I decided to write as well and tell my fans my own inspirational story.'

'So why Kalim? They seem to be under fire for the work they've recently published. You've also been mentioned, in not a very nice way, in these scathing features we've seen lately.' *Ah, here we go.*

'Yes, it's an easy way of getting people's attention, isn't it? Well, I'm not reacting, except to say that Kalim is doing a great job and that all these people who criticize me or their work are those who've tried and failed, and thus have a bone to pick with others who have an audience, so to speak.' *Nice! Low blow.*

'You mean Mr Gaurav Bedi?' Sohail asked with a wry grin. *This guy is good.*

'He's one of them, for sure. You know, I've seen his show, and all he does is put down what is popular with the masses and praise things that no one's heard about, pretending to be intelligent and show that he has taste and intellect. He should stop talking down to people, as no one's really interested in him or his views. The common man doesn't care about what wine he drinks or the poetry he reads to his buddies. They want to be entertained, and that's where I come in.'

'You seem quite brutal on that view,' Sohail smirked.

'I am! I really don't think the man has much going for him these days. He should really relax and save his rants for his drinking buddies. He should stop insulting the *aam aadmi* who spends his hard-earned money to read an entertaining book or watch an entertaining film.' *Oh nice!*

'Yes, that's very snobbish of him, isn't it? He's had a few things to say about you, Akshay.'

'Yes, a lot has changed since his last assessment of me. We've turned down his book since then.'

'Really! That's an interesting piece of news! What's that about?'

'You really don't want to know. With due respect to him, it didn't make sense for us to publish it.'

'Ha ha! So what do you have planned in the future, apart from Roshan's book?'

'Well, we have Vinod Dutta's much-awaited collection of essays called *Bottled Up*. It's about real issues in India and it's going to make an impact.'

'Is this the last book he mentioned?' *Not quite, but we'll make it seem that way.*

'Yes, we hope to get this out very soon. Roshan has kindly agreed to launch it. Anya Malik is releasing a collection of erotic love stories, *Behind Closed Doors*. We have another sci-fi adventure, *Jarez Rio 2030*, which is our next release.'

'Anya Malik with a collection of erotica! This sounds

interesting! Well, we believe Gaurav Bedi was wrong then; it seems like a case of sour grapes. Good luck to both of you, and goodnight,' Sohail said, signing off with a drum roll.

Roshan and I walked out laughing about all that we had said. We had text messages from Zorah, Anya, Sudhir and even Tarun, who was pleased as a punch.

'What is this book you mentioned that I would be launching?' Roshan asked.

'Oh, it's a small thing. This famous children's writer is in coma. It's his last collection of essays on poverty and environment,' I explained with a straight face. *Thanks to my smart swap deal among the various authors.*

'Yeah, it's a good cause, buddy! Let's do it. Great publicity! You should go and work on my speech. Maybe we can launch it from the hospital; I can talk about being a big fan of the children's books.' *This guy should run for elections.*

'Thanks, man! Let's make it big.' *Oh yeah!* I could imagine Gaurav Bedi seething and describing us as crass, arrogant and disrespectful to his gang of oldies, who were sure to write a nice opinion piece or two on Roshan and my interview. We could use the publicity, with all the new releases coming up. I was under fire already with our first two books bombing, thanks to Tarun's misplaced confidence and haphazard efforts, and now, I was ready to kick ass. *Bring it on, man!*

Day 165

 $\mathcal{Z}$ orah and I entered the office groggy-eyed. I had spent several weekends writing and rewriting chapters for Suryakant Joshi's political memoir. In addition, Zorah and I had been putting in long nights with the upcoming launch of the sci-fi tragedy *Jarez Rio 2030* by the great Sudhir. I was up to my ears with last-minute editing changes, things that Sudhir felt were essential to make it 'filmier'. While Zorah had to organize a cover shoot with Roshan Khan, set up events across the country and get the media to show at least lukewarm interest in Sudhir, who was another in the long line of banker- or techie-turned-authors. The papers talked vaguely about Roshan Khan working on adapting Sudhir's upcoming book as a film for his new production company, Empire Features, and it was Zorah and I who'd set the cat amongst the pigeons on that one with the press. The launch was moved last minute from a leading bookstore to a watering hole in the suburbs, with Sudhir trying to go one up on the poor sods who launched their new titles in a bookstore.

Sudhir, through his PR company, was paying a fortune to get 'famous names' to make an appearance along with Roshan

Khan, who made it known that he would unveil the book, and had me write his little speech where he would wax eloquent about Sudhir and his magnum opus.

'It's finally upon us! The most daunting launch of the year,' I said, resting my arm on Zorah's shoulder.

'Yes, it's been unimaginably stressful. I've just managed to organize everything. Sudhir continues to badger me on Twitter.' *That damn twit.* The last three days were spent retweeting everything he posted about his masterpiece on Twitter, as per his kind request and incessant reminders.

'We should just take a break after this one. We also have a spate of launches coming up in a few weeks.'

'I want to take a break now,' she said softly.

'What do you have in mind?'

'Don't know... maybe take a relaxed shower and get under the sheets.' She turned around and smiled dreamily.

'Yeah, why don't you take off? I'll get home shortly after.'

'Really? But what about office?' It was a quiet evening, except for Tarun, who was busy working the phone with distributors, and Mr Samuel, who filled out the odd invoice.

'We deserve some time off. We don't get paid to work 16 hours a day.' I got a Twitter message from Sudhir. 'Xcited abt 2nite'. *I definitely need a break.*

'Okay, see you soon, tiger. Don't be late,' she said, before leaving on the pretext of meeting our art designer. I left a few minutes later and got home just as Zorah was entering the building. We kissed in the elevator, got into a warm shower, and after making love leisurely, crawled under the sheets and collapsed in each other's arms before falling asleep.

I was rudely woken up by Roshan's phone call. 'Khan, I'm

in a meeting, can I call you back?' *Maybe sometime next week!*

'Hey, look, it's important. I might not make it tonight. I haven't been cast as a villain in the new James Bond film. You remember the film I was lobbying to get ... I don't feel like getting out ...' *Don't feel like it? What does he mean? This is important to us!*

'Oh bummer! Sorry to hear that, Khan! But your presence will help build a buzz for the film based on Sudhir's book. You are a big fan of sci-fi, aren't you? I think this can be a big international project where you play the lead and really prove your detractors wrong.' *What a load of crap!* Zorah turned and twisted next to me, disturbed by my conversation on the phone. 'In fact, Sudhir's agent has been speaking to international studios about the adaptation rights, with the book being launched in London and New York simultaneously. I really think this could be a big move for you.'

'That's an idea. These Hollywood chaps didn't like the past few films I've done. They think I was hamming it up; they don't understand our audiences and the fact that our films are larger than life,' he mourned. *Go ahead, blame others for your snooze fests.*

'I think it's for the best. If we can adapt Sudhir's book, you're in a lead in an international film, where you call the shots and make it the way you want, perhaps play up to an international audience.' *I should be in the movie business instead.*

'Yes, it's going to be mind-blowing,' he quipped. *More like mind-fucking, but whatever.*

'See you tonight, yeah, Khan,' I said before hanging up.

The launch later that night was well organized and went swimmingly well for Sudhir. His publicists had made sure that he got a sufficiently well-heeled crowd, mostly business associates, who made polite conversations and enjoyed hanging around the stars. Roshan Khan fawned over the book, describing it as a 'book lover's delight', while Sudhir looked unhappy that he had little opportunity to speak at his own launch as the media kept asking Roshan about his rivalries and the recent fallout with a director friend. While posing with copies of the book next to celebrities, Sudhir was asked to move out of the frame a number of times, while the photographers took pictures of celebrities and Roshan Khan.

The next morning, we were quite anxious looking at the coverage in the leading papers. Most had images of just Roshan Khan and a couple of other celebrities at the launch. A couple of them featured an image of Zorah and me, and of Anya Malik too, who made a brief appearance after being hounded with invites from Sudhir. The coverage looked more like the opening of a new watering hole or the launch of a new line of women's handbags rather than of a mass-market novel.

There was no image of Sudhir in any of the features, and in one, he was cut out of the frame. This was certainly going to affect the sales of *Jared Rio 2030,* as all that was featured in the press were regular Page 3 faces and blurbs on what they were wearing, as opposed to any information or buzz about the book.

We did, however, hope for good sales, thanks to some paid positive reviews that Sudhir had got done, calling the book 'a fantastic debut', 'a thrilling read', 'an edge-of-the-seat adventure' and 'fresh and poignant', as well as advance bulk orders he had placed at leading bookstores through various people fronting his interests to shore up sales of his book. A couple of early reviews had nothing good to say about the book. One wrote about how 'far-fetched and juvenile' the concept seemed, while another critic called it 'confusing and a tad foolish'. Sudhir, after his futile attempt to hit back at critics, looked to promote the book more aggressively.

I woke up with a direct message from Sudhir on Twitter. 'Pls RT all the positive quotes about *Jarez Rio 2030*'.

I sat up to see my phone buzzing again. It was a call from Jaidev Roy, the owner of JR Books, once the sales head of Kalim and now a rival with a business four times our size.

'Hello, congratulations on releasing a new book! I'm hearing a lot about it,' he said, with some restrained enthusiasm. I could feel him seething with jealousy at the other end, as this was a book that he had turned down.

'Thanks, appreciated!'

'Just to update you, I will take the translation rights to this book; the author is talking to me.' *What?*

'That can't be right. We didn't discuss this with Sudhir...' Zorah stirred in bed, motioning me to lie down by tugging at my T-shirt.

'Nothing to discuss, you see. The author holds the rights and it's up to him...' He hung up shortly afterwards.

Zorah and I were speaking about his ways when the phone rang again. It was Tarun on the other end.

'Things are looking very difficult, yaar,' he said, sounding a tad upset.

'What's going on?'

'We are getting mixed reviews for Sudhir's book, yaar. The stores are saying that sales are average and are refusing to pick up more stock. We are under 10,000 copies, while we still have 15,000 copies in stock...'

'What? I sent you a memo to print no more than 10,000 copies.' *What the heck?*

'Yes, but I had dinner with Sudhir last month and he persuaded me to go with higher numbers. He assured me that this will sell out in the opening week.'

'You shouldn't have listened to Sudhir. I mean, this is absolutely absurd, Tarun. I sent you a memo saying that this book is a risk and we should do a smaller run, even 5,000 copies to be safe.'

'I know, yaar. I don't know what Angus is going to do.'

'Tell him exactly what happened.' *Sorry to say but you're fucked!*

Day 174

The mood in office was sombre, with everyone tiptoeing around a tense and frustrated Tarun, who was facing an onslaught from Angus for being overaggressive with sales projections and from the buyers in bookstores who were furious on ceding considerable shelf space to a book that was doing average business at best. I left early from work, with Zorah still working the phones and trying to get publicity for *Jared Rio 2030* and the other two debacles in the recent past. After a nice shower and some scotch on the rocks, I settled in on the couch to listen to Miles Davis while reading Philip Roth's magnificent *Nemesis* in a single sitting.

Zorah came back home at half past ten and appeared a trifle perturbed about something.

'What are you sulking about, sweet love?' I asked, taking her hand and kissing it.

'I don't know, I'm just tired… I… forget it.' It appeared to me that she wanted to get something off her chest but was hesitant to broach the subject.

'No, go ahead, talk to me,' I moved in behind her and wrapped my arms around her waist, kissing her ear.

'It's just that I'm so stressed out and worried about how we're doing. Things are worse than they were, AK. Especially after not coming good post an overhyped release.'

'You should relax. Sudhir's book not doing better than average is not such a bad thing after all.'

She turned around and glared at me with confusion in her eyes.

'Yeah, imagine if Sudhir's book became a #1 bestseller. We would have created a monster. He's already incorrigible without any noteworthy success as a writer. It's a good thing for readers out there, as they're saved from another overbearing writer who is full of himself.'

The downpour outside was getting worse, as it had been raining steadily all day. There was an awkward silence between us after I had said this, and Zorah withdrew from my embrace and went across to the divan opposite from where I was sitting.

'I can't believe you feel that way. I can't stand Sudhir myself but I haven't held back from doing my best to promote and publicize it.'

'Well, I did my best to edit it too, but it was like flogging a dead horse. I'm just being honest and saying that I'm not particularly sad that his book isn't doing any better than it is. It was rubbish anyway and I think it's getting the kind of reception it deserves.' Zorah glared at me with a mix of frustration and disappointment.

'You know, I had a lot of differences with my father but at least he put his heart and soul into everything he published. He stood by what he did, while I don't think any of this makes a difference to you.'

'Zo, my love, you're overreacting. It's not such...'

'It is a big deal, as we might as well believe in what we work night and day for. We could go out of business within the next few months! But I guess this is just a phase for you to coast along till the storm blows over and you then rush back to London!' she yelled, with the thunder and rumbling outside blending well with the sound of her fury. She stormed out of the room before I could respond, shutting the door behind her and forcing me to spend the night twisting and turning on the divan. The next morning, Zorah left for office before I woke up; I heard the door shut and sat up with a splitting head to notice that it was past 9 a.m. already. I called Sita and let her know that I was staying in with an iffy throat.

I was cross with Zorah and spent most of the morning moping around and thinking about the accusations that Zorah hurled on to me. *Did I care enough about Indian literature? Did I want Kalim to succeed? Or did I despise everything I did?*

Conflicted by my thoughts, I decided to read for a bit and dug into author-signed copies that belonged to old Kalim. I picked *Guide* by R.K. Narayan to start with, and after two and a half hours, I read a few chapters of Bapsi Sidhwa's *Tamas*, followed by Kushwant Singh's *Train to Pakistan* and Ruskin Bond's *Delhi's Not Far* between cups of masala chai.

I made a sandwich for lunch and managed to find a dusty old diary among Iqbal Kalim's book collection. Hesitating for a while as I had no intention to pry, I skimmed through the diary where old Kalim had penned his thoughts about his troubled marriage, about Sita who had awakened hidden desires in him, on how he could never marry her as his wife refused to let him go completely, Zorah's mum falling very ill and passing away, the distant relationship with Zorah, which was among his biggest regrets, and numerous notes about the books that had succeeded at Kalim and what had led to their success. While reading this, I realized that Iqbal Kalim deeply cared about what he did and was passionate about every title that Kalim published. Well, at least till the beginning of the new millennium. He'd once sold his Rolex, gifted to him by his father-in-law, to pay the printer an advance for a large print run of Vinod Dutta's first book, *The Sparrows of Shimla*. Iqbal Kalim had gone from school to school in Bangalore, Mumbai, Pune and Delhi to distribute samples and take orders for the book, which was a resounding success. It had been the beginning of the golden period of Kalim's ascent in the publishing world. There was also a page on Jaidev Roy, a street-smart but rogue salesman who was handpicked by Iqbal Kalim to join the sales team when he saw Jaidev push copies of a book to customers at a retail store in Pune. Soon, Jaidev was appointed sales manager, but the relationship turned sour when Iqbal Kalim learnt that Jaidev was pirating copies of Vinod Dutta's book in collusion with the printer and selling these in bulk quantities in Kolkata. Iqbal Kalim had fired him more 20 years ago and threatened him with dire consequences.

My reading was put on a pause when I received a call from Tamanah, who evaluated books from time to time for Kalim. Over a cup of tea, I discussed with her the merits of a book she'd evaluated for us, *Out in the Woods*—a coming-of-age story of a brand manager who recovers from a life-threatening disorder and spends a year travelling to little-known places to find solace and understand himself. In the process, he finds a deeper meaning to life, finds love and gives back to society by doing what he truly believes in.

At the end of the conversation, I agreed that this was a

book that we must do and decided to set up a conference call with Anup Kurien, the author of this title, the following day.

Not realizing how time flew, enjoying the light drizzle outside, I went back to reading *Tamas* with soft music playing over the speakers, when Zorah entered the apartment, wet from hair to toe. We exchanged a few words about work and how our day was while she changed and I made her a cup of coffee. She sat opposite me and sipped slowly from her mug, while I went back to reading my book.

After what might have been an hour, she set down the coffee mug on the side table and moved closer to where I was, closing the book and putting it away, and slowly running her fingers through my hair and kissing the day-old stubble on my cheek. I woke up with a smile, having just dozed off a few minutes ago.

'I was a little rough on you yesterday but...'

'I'm sorry, you were right,' I said, interrupting her. 'If I'm here doing what I do, I might as well care about it a lot more than I have in the past few months.'

'Really?' She rested her head on my shoulders and sighed softly.

'For starters, I'll be less cynical from now.'

'Hmm...I'm going in for a shower. Do you want to join me?' she asked, fixing those intense eyes on me. I put my arm around her and kissed her softly, while the sound of a Spanish ballad reverberated through the room, and the soft drizzle outside turned into a downpour.

Day 187

Sending off Roshan Khan's book to print was quite a feat. He made no fuss about the changes I had made, approving the book and its contents overnight and focusing all his energies on making repeated changes to his three-page acknowledgement note, where prime ministers to spot boys were thanked for supporting his journey in becoming the country's most arrogant and overrated actor. The press caught on with stories of the book, planted items like how Roshan Khan was advising other celebrities on their biographies and how he had been cajoled by organizers to headline the upcoming Indian Literature Festival. Roshan Khan, being the seasoned publicist, took on a hapless and infuriated Gaurav Bedi in the press, casting himself in the role of spokesperson of the common man who weren't interested in Bedi's elitist opinions. A few jobless youth, pumped up with wads of cash and country hooch by Khan's men, even went as far as to burn effigies of Gaurav Bedi outside the TV studio after he called Roshan Khan a 'foolish and crude fellow who probably had his autobiography ghostwritten'. Roshan revelled in the publicity and spent the whole day giving bytes to journalists and gossip-hungry news stations that kept playing up the Roshan Khan–Gaurav Bedi battle of twits.

Zorah was busy working the phone with the designers, chopping and changing designs to upcoming books. I crept in behind her and watched her in the middle of an intense discussion.

'No no, I want the title in a bigger font, and please change this colour. Red really doesn't work; please make it blue, and send it to me soon,' she said before hanging up.

'The *Bottled Up* cover?'

'Yeah, just making final changes. Roshan Khan's cover is done, and I have sent it to print. Have you seen Tarun?'

'No, I haven't. He was supposed to be in to talk about the launch plans. For some reason, Angus wants both of us on a conference call in a couple of hours.'

'Okay, not Tarun?'

'I think not. He's been hopping mad at Tarun about the *Twilight* and *Stems and Petals* disasters. And, of course, the fiasco about *Jared Rio 2030*'s crazy print run.' The first two books had collectively sold fewer than 3,000 copies, and returns kept flowing in for all three books. Sudhir's book had gone backwards on sales, with over 2,000 copies being returned by bookstores in less than a month.

Roshan walked in, showing up as usual without prior notice, this time with a cowboy hat matched with a pair of boots. He embraced Zorah and me warmly, and had us follow him to my cabin. His Man Friday, secretary, photographer and a couple of other journalist types lurked around.

'I came in because I'm being followed around by the tabloids; wanted to show them that I'm working closely with you guys on the release.' *I think this man believes in his own pretentious life.*

'Are you okay with all the changes I made, Khan?'

'Yeah, you made it funny here and there, na? It isn't that important, tell me what kind of advance orders you have?'

'Some 15,000 copies, so we're doing a run of 20,000 copies, to be safe,' Zorah said.

'Oh, that's less. Make it 25,000 copies; I'll pick up 5,000 myself. I can send complementary copies, donate some to NGOs to sell, and the remaining can be given to these kids on the streets who sell pirated books.' *How sweet!*

'Okay, I'll coordinate this with your office,' Zorah said, before his phone rang.

'Yes, Rameshji! I'm really sorry about cancelling on the shoot this weekend. I tore a ligament in my thigh while at the gym. Yes, it's very painful,' he said, winking at me with an impish grin. *What an actor!*

'Maybe next week. Don't worry, yaar. I'll do it for sure. My office will call you,' he said, before hanging up.

'Are you okay, Khan?' I asked, as Zorah looked at him with disgust.

'*Haan,* yaar! This silly advertisement I was to shoot for. Now I've got this gig to dance at Ankush Malhotra's daughter's wedding. It's very good money. The ad film can wait, hai na?' he smirked.

'Who is going to be there for your launch?'

'Zorah, don't worry, baby. Half a dozen Bollywood actresses who can't wait to work with me and also three to four directors will be there. It will be a big event; I would prefer the Marriott but I agree with your point of keeping it down to earth. Instead, we'll have a nice exclusive after-party at Red Light.'

Zorah frowned, and I jumped in, 'Yeah, it'll be a blast.'

'Thanks, I'm going to see you guys soon at the pre-release bash at Olive. Let's get some pictures taken before I leave.'

He pulled me aside and whispered, 'I'm getting some fillers and some work on my eyebrows done.' He walked away after posing with his arrogant smirk plastered on his face, and I already began to visualize news item releases talking about advance copy sales of the autobiography.

Soon afterwards, another uninvited guest, Sudhir, walked into my cabin looking upset. *Someone please find him a shrink!*

'So I'm still getting tough love, Akshay?' he said, sitting down opposite me. 'Sales are in the bloody dumps. Some jobless hacks are writing scathing reviews and putting them up online.'

'Hi Sudhir! Yes, it's been rather difficult, hasn't it? But I do think your publicity is rather good. At least people know you as a writer now.'

'Not too well. Despite my publicist's efforts, all I'm hearing about is Roshan Khan's book every single day. Even the upcoming launch of that old man Vinod Dutta's book is being talked about.' *Great, we've been doing a swell job.*

'That's wonderful, isn't it? Vinod Dutta deserves to get his due.'

'I don't care, man! I've decided to write a prequel and sequel to my book. I've also decided to let JR Books publish them. There isn't much interest with you here…' *I don't care about the sequel or the prequel, but it will be horrible for us if word gets out on this development.*

'Oh, that's really unfortunate. Maybe I'll tell Zorah to not request Roshan to block his dates for a discussion about a film adaptation. I was just talking to him about how your book has the potential for a film. He wants you at his launch party,' I said, stressing on some of the words and keeping a straight face.

'Really? Roshan wants me at his party?'

'He'll even throw a success party for you, and if you don't irritate him, maybe even the film will happen.' *Learning the game, ain't I?*

'You should do the sequel and prequel then, man. Sorry yaar, I had no clue.'

'Yes, it's an interesting idea. You should go away for a few months, sit undisturbed on some island and just focus on writing them.' *And never come back. May you get swept away—or bitten by a crab, at least.*

'That's a good idea. Yes, I can go away for a few weeks…'

'A man needs some peace and solitude to write. You can't do that in Mumbai while being on Twitter all the time. Try to plan for a writing retreat for at least three months.'

'Yes, let me plan something,' he said contemplatively before leaving.

Zorah joined me soon after and we rang Angus, who seemed aloof and pissed off.

'Guys, I have news for you. I fired Tarun this morning.'

'What?'

'Yes, he's made a shamble of things and he doesn't understand a damn thing about books. He's been getting into scraps with bookstores and the media. I had to put a stop to him banging on about how everyone's an asshole.' *End of the buy-two-get-one-free offers.*

'What do we do now?'

'We have a guy, Rohit Bakshi, from JR Books, who quit after differences with the management. He's young and has put in the years. I've asked Rohit to manage sales and improve relationships with trade and distribution.'

I realized that Angus had seen the writing on the wall and had been working behind the scenes. Getting Rohit onboard was a master stroke.

'We're up against the wall after the failure of these two books that Tarun pushed. Printing excessive copies of Sudhir's book has also damaged us; we have printer bills to clear and dead stock piling up.'

'Rohit has experience and Tarun will no longer be in the way acting like an imbecile. Zorah and you have the freedom to push this forward.' *Yeah, go ahead, blame that sorry bastard. You hired him in the first place.*

'Yes, but you need to cut us some slack; we had no one for a while and then we had Tarun...' Zorah said, the frustration in her voice going through clearly.

'I'm aware, but, Akshay and Zorah, here's the thing. If we can't turn this thing around in six months, we'll have to wrap this up and commission our catalogue to someone else.' *Oh blimey!*

'I think we have three promising books, but we need time, Angus. We've done some damage with the first three,' I chipped in.

'I don't think so, mate. The targets are the same—five serious bestsellers—and we have a little less than six months. I don't think I can convince my old man to give us more time.'

'We need more money for marketing. It's impossible for a small team like ours to do what you expect of us. At the end of the day, even the three books we've done have sold more than what Kalim had done for the past three years. I do believe you need to loosen up a bit and support us a lot more with marketing budgets.' I sounded angry and defiant, and hoped Angus would go on the defensive, as he wouldn't risk firing the Managing Editor hours after getting rid of the CEO.

'It's going to be difficult. I can't promise you...'

'In that case, I can't promise you much either. You can fire all of us if you like. But if we had twice the marketing budget, we could have some chance at success, considering all the bookstores are pissed off with Tarun's antics.'

'Fine, you'll get your budget—and you'll get me results. Else, you can stay back in India, mate. If we don't get this done, the imprint in London won't happen.'

'I understand,' I said, smiling at Zorah, who squeezed my arm.

'We'll do what we can!' Zorah said, beaming from ear to ear.

'Great! All the best! Tarun will be in tomorrow, please take a handover from him, Akshay. Rohit should also join in a day or two. You're the Managing Editor and CEO going forward.'

Wait, I'm the boss now?

'In this case, make sure I have a say in hiring decisions. You can't impose people on me and expect me to deliver, as I need to build a team I can work with.' There was silence at the other end for a minute and all we heard was static coming through.

'I'm sorry, mate, I will. You're right, I'll make sure you have the last word,' he said sheepishly before he hung up.

We continued sitting there after the call. Zorah's phone buzzed with a text from a journalist: 'Vinod Dutta is seriously ill, may not last too long.'

'Zorah, how are we on his cover? Can we send this to print?'

'Yes, we can. Do you want to push this before Roshan's book? I think we can convince him!' *The girl has a point...*

'Yes, we're in trouble otherwise. Let this new guy come in

tomorrow; let's send it out to print. You should start all your publicity efforts. I'll talk to Roshan and tell him that we'll do this one as a build-up to his launch.'

'When do you want to launch it, then?'

'Two to three weeks from now! I don't think we can waste any time. Let's get enough stock of his old books as well.'

'Yes, we have new illustrative covers for them. Let me go and chat with the printer,' she said as she got up to leave. I watched her walk out of the cabin as I pushed the buttons to dial Roshan Khan's unlisted number. *Battle for survival begins!*

Day 188

Tarun walked into a buzzing office with a frown on his face. He was unshaven and looked depressed, with his bloodshot eyes, khaki kurta and a pair of faded jeans. It felt like he was likely to vandalize the place, given the frustration on his face. Zorah said a polite 'hi and good luck' and went back to preparing for the launch. Sita ignored him, given her contempt for him, and Mr Samuel continued to read the newspaper—he had some respite from someone standing over his shoulder and demanding that he make sales calls. I walked up to Tarun and greeted him cheerfully.

'This is not good, yaar. I get blamed because bookstores are lazy,' he groaned.

'I understand, this is a tough business. Those two were difficult books to sell, really. And that Sudhir's book—readers are already complaining to bookstores—was a risky proposition; maybe playing it safe would've worked...' *I told you so.*

'I thought we could sell 20,000 to 25,000 copies with an aggressive promotion strategy.' *Sorry mate, you bet on the wrong horses. In fact, you bet on mules.*

'I'm sorry it had to end this way.'

'My life is a mess. Three years back, when I was heading

sales for the ice cream division, I had so many offers, and a promising career. The energy drinks division that I led didn't quite succeed, and now this.'

'So what's next for you?' I asked, patting his back and taking him into my office.

'I don't know, yaar! I can't even look at my wife and my son. I haven't told them yet. I said I'm on a break as the company is having financial trouble. Where can I go now? I don't want to work for someone like Roshan Khan, he's too moody.' *Or too stoned most of the time.*

'I have a contact for you. Nikita Mishra, this lady from the UK whom I met at Roshan's party, she's an art collector. She wants to set up a gallery here in Mumbai and basically showcase her collection, maybe auction some work, as well as bring in new-age art by young artists in Europe.'

'That's very nice, but like books, I have no experience in all this. She'll remove me after six months for the same reason.'

'No, don't worry. She wants someone to kind of manage the gallery: host events, run the place. She also needs someone smart and aggressive with sales experience. I think you could do it,' I said, egging him on.

'Here, why don't you call her? She's keen to do this soon,' I said, writing the number for him and leading him out of my cabin towards the exit.

'Thanks, Akshay! If I get the job, it'll save my life, yaar. I tell you, you should find another job too. You've become a celebrity. What are you doing here?' *Good question.*

'I'll fight it out till I can,' I said, gazing at Zorah admirably as she worked the phone.

'You're in love, eh? I know...'

'Good luck with Nikita, I hope it works out,' I said, keeping my gaze fixed on Zorah, as Tarun picked up his box of personal belongings and memorabilia and headed for the exit.

Rohit got into work that afternoon and began to look depressed and confused about his move after a quick briefing by Zorah and me.

'It's like starting from scratch; things are pretty bad with the sales set-up here,' he said. *It's the pre-Independence era, mate.*

'Yeah! When I got in, there were no computers. Look, I had to build things from scratch when I got here. I've had a few months; you, unfortunately, have little time before the next launch.'

'Yes, I better get to it then. It's going to be a rollercoaster ride,' he said with a raised brow. *That's an understatement, if there was one.*

'It sure is,' I grinned.

'Who is that uncle reading the newspaper?'

'He's all the sales and production staff you have. He knows everything, latch on to him,' I said. *Mr Samuel is the man.*

'He seems to be leaving...' Rohit said, looking worried.

'Yeah, he leaves by 3 p.m. It's time for his afternoon nap. He's sort of a part-time employee.' *Who doesn't get paid!*

'Oh well, alright! He's kind of old. I'll talk to him in the morning.'

Sita came knocking on my door at the end of the day.

'I wanted to have a word with you.'

'Sure...' *Are you quitting? Because we can get someone who actually works.*

'I'm a little worried with the way things are going. In the past, we never had books that we published coming back from stores the way they are,' she said, looking spooked.

'There's a learning curve. With Rohit here, I think things will be better.'

'But Angus had said we only have one year. Now there are only six months remaining and we need five books on the bestseller lists.' *You've done the math, lady!*

'Sure, it's going to be a challenge, and we need all the support you can give us.'

'I want to support you, Akshay! This is my home. I've spent all my working life in this firm. I don't want to see it shut down,' she said, with a desperate look in her eyes. *Well, now you can actually begin working.*

'Rohit will need all the support he can possibly get. He has a lot to do to get sales systems and production in place. You could get on and support more of his work, and help Mr Samuel. I don't think he can manage by himself…'

'Sure, anything you tell me to. I want us to survive.'

'I do too, and we are all on the same team. To make this a success is why I'm here,' I said with a confident nod. She smiled at me reassuringly and crept out. *That wasn't bad!*

I got a text from Tarun: 'I got the job. I start setting up next week! Thank you, yaar!' *Well, good luck peddling art, buddy! Maybe three for the price of two will work better in the art business. Maybe not. Go figure.*

Day 201

The days leading up to the launch of Vinod Dutta's book *Bottled Up* were intense and stressful for everyone involved. The actual authors, Sandeep and Shipra, whose book it really was, were credited in the book as co-writers and researchers. They were very supportive by actively getting involved and helping Zorah with the launch and marketing efforts. The pre-publicity efforts were perfectly pitched with Roshan and a number of celebrities—most of them friends of Roshan whom I often partied with—talking to the media about their favourite memories linked with Vinod Dutta's earlier books, with most of them reading blurbs to the media that Zorah and I had written. The next day this was followed by the release of one of the essays on displacement of tribal settlements and degrading of the environment, which led to a number of activists and *jholawallas* commenting on it in the next few days.

Accompanied by an enthused group of photographers and journalists, Roshan Khan and a leading environment activist, Somesh Jha, a copy of the new book was placed on the table next to Vinod Dutta's hospital bed, as he lay there in a trance, awake but delirious, possibly with his mind having already departed to another world. Zorah and I stood aside nervously, as photographers clicked the copy of the book and had to be persuaded not to create a disturbance as they quizzed us about the contents and the importance of the book.

Later that evening, Roshan Khan, looking dapper in a black suit, unveiled the 'highly relevant' book by his 'childhood hero' to a large audience that included business, entertainment and books journalists who were swayed by the buzz the book had created.

This was followed by Anya reading an excerpt from two essays—one on poverty alleviation and the other on education in rural areas. She added her opinion on these subjects by agreeing with Vinod Dutta's assessment of the situation and by impressively throwing across statistics and figures at the stunned audience, who were more inclined to dig into samosas and puffs, and sip wine at these book launches. Sandeep and Shipra took questions from the audience and spoke about the process of writing the book, just as we had coached them, as a team effort between them and Vinod Dutta. They also revealed their plans to do a second set of essays on the subject, just as Vinod Dutta had wanted, and confirmed that Kalim was to publish this.

The press coverage that followed the next morning was beyond our wildest belief. Suryakant Joshi, the former education minister, who had been given an advance copy, wrote a piece where he described the book as 'brave and hugely relevant for anyone with an interest to improve the lives of our people'. He called upon the government to pay heed to the recommendations and suggestions mentioned in the book.

The hospital saw a flurry of activity, and Vinod Dutta's

caretaker Ramu received VIP guests and ministers, who came to see the 'great' author and 'inspiring human being', and spoke with sad faces about how he might never recover.

The Prime Minister, hearing about the buzz surrounding the book, jumped into the action, asking all officers and administrators in the government to read the book and recommending the 'brave and realistic' suggestions of a 'wonderful human being'. Vinod Dutta was, of course, oblivious to the praise and recognition for the book he hadn't written, while Shipra and Sandeep were over the moon, landing assignments to write columns for newspapers and to serve on committees to resolve some of the issues they'd written about. Sales soared and the phones never stopped ringing. Rohit, who had been thrown in at the deep end, spent sleepless nights getting thousands of copies across the country. Enthusiastic kids decided to organize a candle march for Vinod Dutta's recovery and leading editors wrote about how they were 'positively surprised by the courageous final book' by a great author.

A week after its release, the book stood at #1 on the non-fiction national bestseller list, with over 100,000 copies sold in bookstores and online. Angus was delighted and managed to sell the rights in the European and American markets to Falcon Books, the world's largest, for $500,000, most of which went to Sandeep and Shipra, given the agreement we had struck. The President strolled in one stormy evening, with a delegation of literary hangers-on and foreign ambassadors and emissaries, to see Vinod Dutta, whom he described as a 'warm and passionate soul'.

The tailwind was with us and it appeared like we had turned the corner. Roshan threw a fundraiser party to celebrate the success of the book, where Anya Malik, whom the tabloid media had begun speculating as Vinod Dutta's former protégé and muse, was one of the bartenders.

Nine days after the launch, Jaidev Roy, the owner of JR Books, dressed in a cheap navy blue suit, dropped in for a visit.

'So it's wonderful news on the success of your new book! I really liked the cover,' he said, gritting his teeth and rubbing his paunch. He was an evil-looking man with yellow teeth, the shifty gaze of a lowlife thug and hair on the sides combed over to cover his bald patch at the centre. He proudly put down his new iPad and two smartphones on the table, and fidgeted with the rings on his fingers.

'Thank you, I preferred what was in the book.' *You, of course, are too dense to understand it.*

'Oh, I don't think so. You can't agitate against progress and enterprise. We have to support industrialists and bring foreign investment to encourage growth. There has to be a compromise when we need growth and development, hai na?' B*loody shark!*

'One has to balance these interests and keep in mind the environment and the have-nots as well.'

'It seems like you're a big supporter of what the book says,' he frowned with raised brows.

'I absolutely agree with most of what it says.'

'You know, there's something that worries me about the book. A lingering thought that refuses to go away,' he said, looking at me carefully and smiling to himself.

'And what is that?'

'Shipra Tewari was talking about wanting to write a book on the very same issues over a year back. I tried to dissuade her, given that youngsters want to read love stories and not about poverty and environmental problems. I can see that she's very involved with this book,' he said with a weak grin.

'She is one of the co-writers and led a lot of the research. She believes in the issues and she's a crusader for a good cause. She's done valuable research for the book,' I said, looking at him in the eyes.

'She's a crusader for a good cause or the real author of this communist propaganda? I don't believe the scotch- and cigar-loving Vinod Dutta had the inclination, the temperament or the presence of mind to actually write about these issues. The man was a compulsive skirt chaser in his heydays who lived a colourful life and certainly didn't give a damn about the environment. I've even heard he used to do a bit of hunting.'

'You're making some wild accusations, Jaidev,' I said in a calm voice.

'I might have an email from Shipra. The brief synopsis in that and the contents of this book are strikingly similar.' *Oh you damn son of a ....*

'Yes, and after she pitched the concept around and it didn't work out, she persuaded Mr Dutta—a great writer, as you know—to write the book, providing him with, as I mentioned, valuable research.' I smiled.

'I may want to send this email to the media, let them draw their own conclusions. What do you say? I think a lot of people will be upset and embarrassed if this got out,' he said with a laugh.

'I don't know why that's necessary. You'll be insulting a great man on his death bed.' *Time to start looking for a job if this happens.*

'Well, let's see. I can reconsider and forget about it if you give me the other Indian-language translation rights at a small fee.' *What a snake! You turned this book down, you constipated moron!*

'It's difficult, but let me talk to my team…' *I'd rather break your skull with my paperweight.*

'It will be in your best interests,' he snarled, showing off his expensive gold watch as he picked up his phones and the iPad and walked out of my cabin. I sat there for a while, too stunned by what had just happened, thinking about the implications of him knowing what he knew.

I summoned Zorah in for a meeting, pulling her out of another set of interview questions she was responding to from the media.

Day 214

$\mathcal{I}$ was up early, thinking about the reminder I had received
from Jaidev Roy. There were already a couple of murmurs by
journalists from Gaurav Bedi's camp about how Vinod Dutta
was a lover of Jack Daniel's and younger women, and had no
communist leanings or any particular interest in the environment
or Indian society. They were taken on in social media by other
young writers and journalists, and described as 'corporate
stooges' and 'unscrupulous sellouts'.

A Left-leaning political party was planning to build a statue
of Vinod Dutta, and his hospital room was thronged by visitors
and sympathizers who saw him as a man who cared about the
common lot.

'What are we going to do about this Jaidev Roy problem?'
Zorah asked, turning around and resting her head on my chest.
My head was filled with anxieties about the launch of Roshan's
Khandom tonight.

'Hmm...I've been stalling him. Let's talk about it after the
launch of Roshan's book tonight.' *Yes, the upcoming firecracker.*
The book had already climbed to #2 behind Vinod Dutta's book
as a bestseller, just on the basis of advance orders, mostly from

Roshan himself and his cronies.

'That was a wily move, swapping the authors on the book. But what are we going to do with Vinod Dutta's erotic novel? Surely you're not going to get Anya...'

'Of course I am, and she's agreed to do it. She loves the publicity and likes being in the limelight. I want you to arrange a nice photoshoot for her. We'll send the images to leading papers and magazines.' *This is almost like the release of an adult film.*

'Hmm...yes, I can arrange it once Archana, Roshan's publicist, gets off my back. She's been on my case with Roshan's book.'

'Yeah, I can imagine how excited he is. We've had a week of back-to-back parties to celebrate the success of his book.'

'I know, it's funny! I've never seeing so much hype and undue attention in the launch of a book.'

'Yes, well, did you send in those bits from the book late last night? I want these journalists to read those snippets.'

'Yeah, I did! These guys were excited about it. This book is creating a buzz,' she said, holding on to me tighter.

'Yep, it's going to be fun tonight.' *For us, at least!*

Roshan Khan, in a black tuxedo, quite stoned and with an arm around the budding starlet in his new film, entered the bookstore two hours later than the launch was intended to begin, and was mobbed by ardent fans—possibly those his team had found or paid to be there—and the paparazzi. The literary crowd ignored the event and simply didn't show up, except for a couple of senior entertainment journalists who were often hanging around in his parties. Soon after he had passed a couple of his witty wisecracks about the traffic and the humid weather, we settled in for a round of questions and answers with the media.

The first hand went up, and a bespectacled woman journalist grabbed the microphone. 'Did you really help Abhijit Rana with his English dialogues in the film you did together?' *Here's the first of the doosras.* Roshan looked amused and smiled at his leading lady, who giggled. Abhijit was a 50-plus actor who was now down and out, struggling with small parts and cameos in big-budget films.

'Yes, he's a nice man. Everyone isn't a native English speaker and, funnily, he was playing the role of a man living in London. I did support him with his dialogues, as when you make a film it's a selfless process. You have to support the rest of the cast and crew...'

'He says you shouted and argued with him and the director because he didn't get his lines right.' The grin was wiped off Roshan's face with this accusation.

'No, this isn't true. We do argue on set but often it is a constructive approach to improving things.'

'Sorry, but you've also mentioned in the book that you helped out director Anil Rathore in his debut film. You wrote about how you gave him tips on directing actors and sorting out problems he had with his cast and crew,' another journalist said, reading from her notes.

'Yes, with newcomers, I like to get involved and support them as much as I can...' Khan smiled as he slurred a bit through his monologue, and the starlet looked coy and turned a shade of pink. *More like throw your weight around and take over the making of the film. Unless, of course, it's a girl...*

'But that's not the version that Anil gives us. He's said that you were constantly late, lazy and uncooperative, and thanks to you, his production schedule and budget went completely haywire. He cites a situation where you showed up, shot for one dialogue and asked for the crew to pack up for the day. He also says you refused to promote the film,' the journalist added, and there was muffled laughter in the room as Roshan looked agitated.

'That's not what he said at the press conference of his premiere, right? Anil shouldn't blame his failures on me. His last film with the opposite camp also did just average business. He's upset because I refused the last subject he approached me with. I wish him all the best.'

'You also wrote fondly about your bonding a lot and partying with Sunil Panda and Suhnaina Shetty on your last feature film, *Beijing*. You've mentioned that you were "inseparable buddies" and that they were "quite the lovey-dovey couple during the making of the film",' the journalist continued. Roshan looked around to catch my eye but I crept quietly behind the bookshelf, avoiding his twitching gaze. One night over drinks, he had jokingly spoken about how the two actors were busy snogging each other while they played brother and sister in the film.

'Yes, they are very sweet people. That's just a joke between us friends; I wrote that in jest as I often joked with them about being a nice-looking couple. Unfortunately, the film didn't work, but I look forward to working with them again,' he said, stuttering a bit and looking uncomfortable.

'We contacted the actors and this is what they had to say. Sunil says that you had his "scenes chopped" and asked him to "play it gay" in order to put your character into focus. Suhnaina says, "I barely interacted with either of them during the shoot. I happen to know Sunil for a while but I don't know what Roshan is going on about". Roshan looked visibly annoyed and fidgety, and the lissome lass sitting next to him decided to text on her phone and pretend that nothing was going on, while photographers clicked away.

'I think it's quite late, just three more questions,' his publicist Archana barked. 'Yes, you,' she said handing the microphone to a young journalist at the back of the room.

'Are you and Rahim Khan having problems? You've said, "His dog, Bruno, would be better at picking scripts; he just gets lucky with duds becoming hits while I work very hard." How do you think he'll react to this?' Roshan looked petrified and almost ducked for cover.

'I'm just kidding, obviously; my friends will understand my sense of humour. I'm very fond of Rahim and his pug, Bruno...'

'We hear that he is very upset and he's no longer doing a cameo in your film after hearing these comments,' the young journalist continued, as Roshan Khan looked grave, like he wanted to make a dash for it.

'You've written, "The industry is filthy, with a lot of sleaze, backbiting, big egos and power struggles. All those rumours you hear are true, people lack courage to speak." Don't you think that's a bold statement? Most industry bigwigs find this comment insulting and demeaning,' an elderly newspaper reporter asked.

'Er... well... sometimes there is a problem and it's good to talk about them...' Roshan said, trying to brave a smile. Archana stepped in to rescue him again, 'Okay, last question for the night.' *After all the hammering!*

'You've written that you get many international offers that you've turned down. You've said the Philip David and John McGregory had offered you lead roles. Mr David says he only briefly met you at a party and that you didn't discuss any film, nor has he considered you. Mr McGregory claims that you contacted him offering to play the role of a cab driver in his film. What really happened?' a leading journalist who was friends with Gaurav Bedi asked.

'Philip and I discuss a lot of ideas, although I admit nothing was concrete. He's upset because I haven't returned his call recently. John McGregory and I seem to be getting prank calls from someone who is imitating us on the phone. I absolutely haven't called McGregory,' he said, looking flustered as he stood up to brave a smile for the shutterbugs. 'Why the hell would I call some Indie filmmaker offering to play a bit part in a festival film when I'm inundated with scripts?' He literally stormed out of the bookstore, followed by journalists and cameramen who thrust their microphone and cameras in his face.

'One more question,' a journalist shouted. 'You said that Istanbul is your favourite holiday destination and that you went there recently on a holiday with actress Supriya Sharma. Please comment.' His publicist chided the journalist while Roshan's Audi Q6 sped away in a hurry as photographers clicked on and huddled around afterwards to smoke and share a laugh or two about the press conference they'd just witnessed.

Day 216

After making a brief appearance at his own party and then not showing up for the rest of the night, word was that Roshan Khan had gone underground. I couldn't get through his phone all of yesterday and he failed to respond to any of my messages. The media had a field day with a full page in the tabloid section of papers with what the book said, what the people concerned had to say about it tweets by a number of celebrities who took sides with one or the other, and Roshan Khan's comments, some witty and most others defensive, at the launch. Jobless half-celebrities, who often commented at every given opportunity, couldn't hold back this time either. Gaurav Bedi described Roshan Khan's book as 'full of lies', power broker and lobbyist Pushkar Premnath described it as a 'vulgar attempt at cheap publicity. Roshan Khan should be castrated.' Bestselling novelist Sampat Vidhyarti described it as 'a comical book I wouldn't write.' While Ramesh Nath, controversial film director and full-time spokesperson on celebrity scandals, described it as a 'brave and honest account of the industry'. A number of glamour haters and Leftists took up for Khan and called him 'courageous' and a 'real man', while a number of starlets who wanted to work with him cooed about how 'real' and 'funny' the book was and how they 'loved it'. It didn't matter that ostensibly none of these people could have possibly bought copies on the evening of the launch and finished the book in time to comment on Twitter and be quoted in the papers the next morning. But all the buzz and controversy had given a fillip to sales: the book, despite its price of ₹695 in hardcover, began to outsell every other book that released that week and topped the new releases charts on all online bookstores.

The morning had started with a bang, with headlines and images of Rahim Khan showing up at Roshan's sea-facing penthouse in Juhu in an inebriated state and challenging him to a fight outside. There was talk of him kicking the gate of Roshan's building and trying to climb the walls, before Roshan Khan's wife managed to placate him and send him away. There was a feature where battle lines were drawn and camps were divided between the warring Khans.

Gaurav Bedi took up for Rahim Khan in an interview with a news channel, describing his actions as 'emotional' while stating that Roshan had written things that were 'ludicrous and in bad taste'. Anil Rathore, who was planning a film with both the Khans in the lead, had now shelved the project and said he was 'unlikely to work with Roshan Khan ever'. There was one favourable planted piece that mentioned fans standing outside Roshan Khan's house and waiting for the superstar to sign copies for them. It said that Roshan Khan was delirious and excited about the 'fabulous' response to his book.

Zorah and I got into work early, responding to questions from the media on the recently launched book and on the continued interest and buzz around Vinod Dutta's book. While discussing a specific response to a leading journalist on Anya's upcoming novel, we noticed an angry-looking Archana and a weary-eyed Roshan Khan enter our office. Roshan walked in and smiled feebly before greeting Zorah and me with his trademark hug. He collapsed on the chair, looking like he hadn't slept in days and Archana took a seat next to him and frowned at both of us, given how we had stalled on giving her an advance copy of the book till a couple of minutes before the launch.

'Fuck, what did you guys end up doing? You guys are nuts,' he said, looking exhausted and a tad stoned.

'Khan, we sent the book to you with all the changes marked. It was sent to the printer only after you okayed everything,' Zorah said in a business-like tone. *Yeah, you were probably too high to read any of it.*

'Yeah, I didn't read any of it, and thank God for that,' he said with his trademark smirk.

'I mean this is fucking amazing! This Archana and her team have been doing shit for years. Making me throw brunches, tea parties and after-parties, getting clicked with race horses, corporate types and cricketers, and planting silly stories no one gives a shit about.' Archana looked gutted and shuffled uncomfortably in her seat. *What the… !*

'I mean this is kick-ass phenomenal coverage! My phone hasn't stopped ringing with all the publicity. Yeah, I need to watch my back with Rahim Khan for a while—that was a bit nasty—but I've been flooded with offers for six new films,' he grinned and sat back with a pompous air about him. 'And—hold your breath—a cameo of sorts in a new Netflix series being shot in Istanbul.'

Zorah and I looked at each other with surprise and some

relief. We had some fear of being sued but this was spiralling into something else.

'The sales are phenomenal, Khan. Congratulations! This is going to become an all-time bestseller,' I said. He looked proud and had tears in eyes, with that cocky smirk plastered on his face.

'What awesome publicity! You're my best buddy,' he said, and embraced me. *Okay, get off me. What are we, in high school?*

'We're so happy for you, Khan! You're the rockstar,' Zorah chirped. *Okay, we're kind of overdoing it now.*

'Okay guys, I'm inclined to say yes to two or three of those projects I've been offered. It's good money, but it's run-of-the-mill, you know. I want to green-light something on my own. I know this is sudden, but got any ideas?' *Oh! We have many. The Jackass of Juhu, for starters. Why not make a movie about yourself?*

'We'll let you know...' Zorah began, when I interrupted.

'There is this futuristic superhero theme, Khan. You'd be perfect for it. Sudhir, whom you've met, has authored it. You were at his launch too. Best part is, he's also writing a sequel and prequel to the novel.' *A film deal will sell the book.*

'Superhero film—that's a bit ambitious, isn't it?' *Just like you writing a book, mate.*

'Khan, you'd be portrayed as this invincible demi-god. I think it's great; it hasn't been attempted, and I'm helping him write this one. The aim is to make it look and feel like an international film.' *Massage the ego, that'll do it.*

'That's the idea! Something mind-blowing, where I'm invincible! Man, you're just amazing,' he said, shaking my hand. 'You guys should pop by for dinner and a drink tonight, let's talk. I've got to rush off to a press conference outside my house.'

Ah, the theatrics continue.

We watched the news later, where Khan spoke eloquently to the media, talking about how he'd been honest to himself and in certain places 'took liberties and wrote in jest' about a few of his friends. He mentioned how 'taken aback' he was by Rahim Khan's behaviour and described Gaurav Bedi as 'a frustrated old man picking a fight to get some attention', Sunil Panda as a 'jealous struggler' and quoted how he'd done him 'favours' and got him 'supporting roles' where he played the lead. He also touched upon some lofty ambitious projects he was planning, including an 'adaptation' of an 'exciting book'. The media was enthralled by his ready wit and his sharp quips when he defended the book confidently, laughed off some embarrassing bits and even had a word of praise for me and Zorah for encouraging him to 'tell my story like it is'. We switched channels to see another item that caught our eye: 'Vinod Dutta—hero of the masses—in critical condition.'

Zorah and I left for the hospital and were soon joined by Anya and a number of other authors and journalists, including Shipra and Sandeep. A grief-stricken Ramu stood quietly by the door, and a few politicians, celebrities and even Roshan Khan made fleeting visits to make the most of the photo opportunity. Suryakant Joshi declared to the media that Vinod Dutta's vital contribution couldn't be ignored and promised to open a school in his village in the memory of the great writer who was battling for his life. The same night, at half past nine, Vinod Dutta breathed his last, unaware of his status as the country's #1 bestselling author, with a final book released in his name, although it wasn't the one he'd written.

I looked at his limp body lying on the hospital bed and

rushed out of the room overcome by emotion. *I promise you it'll be out soon.*

Zorah and I left the hospital shortly after his passing, not wanting to be dragged into the media circus, with writers, ministers and everyone hungry for a mention quoting how they had been 'saddened by the loss'. We skipped the offer to have dinner and drinks with Khan and instead had a quiet meal at Café Churchill, where I spoke fondly of the time I'd spent with the old man over cups of tea and glasses of scotch, before heading back home.

Day 244

$\mathcal{I}$ was flooded with invitations to various events and competitions. From a small-time reality show to college events, the office was flooded with requests for me to step in and judge, make an appearance or give a lecture. With some encouragement from Zorah and the realization that I had to get out there and mingle with and understand the youth, I took up an offer to judge a personality contest at a women's college that catered to the low-income group in Chennai. This is where I met Shweta Iyer, a talented, dusky beauty who was a former beauty-pageant winner and a popular youth icon who ran a dance academy and her own theatre company, apart from featuring in a couple of hard-hitting Tamil films. We caught up over a cup of coffee after the contest and she told me about a book she was writing called *Dance into Life*, which was about her journey to growing into a confident and successful woman. In her teenage years, she was overweight and unattractive by her own admission and realized when she was among the only girls at a high school prom in Nainital that she had to do something for herself beyond getting good grades. She was absolutely ignored by the boys, without being asked to dance by even one of them. She went away to

Yale Law College in New York, where her father was a college professor, and took up dance classes, working intensively on herself. By the end of the year, she had dropped out of college and was teaching ballet, jazz and ballroom dancing at the academy before she participated in Miss India, resisting opposition from her father, and emerged as the second runner-up. She was wondering if I could read her manuscript and give her my feedback. She was delighted when I agreed, and managed to have her assistant print it and bring to the airport where I was scheduled to be in a couple of hours. I spent a couple of hours reading her manuscript, which was an easy, breezy read with a simple and engaging narrative. I got off the flight thinking about the thousands of men and women who would draw inspiration from this journey. I called Shweta on my way to office and said that this was a book that we had to publish, convincing her that we would keep the story intact and work around tightening the edit and helping her elevate the quality of the writing. She agreed immediately and said, 'Only because I trust you much more than the publishers out there, who are simply chasing their bottom lines.'

'You won't regret it,' I said, signing off.

I got into office after an hour and was given the messages Jaidev Roy had left with Sita, asking me to return his calls at the earliest. I did just that.

'We'll have to really think about and discuss your demands about the rights you requested,' I said carefully.

'Demands, is it? I've been asked to join Gaurav Bedi in a debate on the future of publishing. Maybe I'll talk about your little switching of authors in that forum.'

'Be my guest.' *Someone please shoot this guy.*

'It will be scandalous, I tell you. It will take you down, such a shame. So much potential...'

'Look, I've said we'll get back to you. There's no need to make additional demands.'

'Don't get upset, Akshay. We should be friends, you see. Let's do one thing, let's forget this story.'

'And?'

'Why don't you send me some good material worth publishing? Maybe you can come join us in six months and bring that girlfriend of yours with you.' *Ah, so that's what you're after!*

'So let's get this right. You want me to take apart what I've built, and come and work for you?'

'Sure, I can offer you more than what you get paid there,' he guffawed.

'You can go to hell!'

'Well, I'd like those rights worked out in the next few weeks. I'm on Gaurav Bedi's *Books Talk* next month,' he said angrily.

'We'll think about it,' I said, before hanging up and heading over to Zorah's workstation to speak to her about Shweta's book.

The next morning, my phone buzzed shortly after 7 a.m. It was Rahul Nanda, an upcoming literary agent based in Delhi who practically worked 20 hours a day. He had flown in all the way from the capital to meet me last week and begin a working relationship.

'Hi, AK! Do you have a minute to talk?'

'Sure,' I said, glancing at my sleeping seductress, Zorah.

'There is this hilarious novel by a college kid in Bengaluru, are you interested?'

'Have you shown it to anyone else?'

'To be honest, it's been rejected by everyone. But I think it's bloody fantastic.'

'Who is this by?'

'Sunil Kumar, a college kid, who works part time in a leading bookstore.'

'Interesting… Has Jaidev Roy seen it?'

'He's a nut job, man. He rejects anything good I send him and instead has a taste for the usual garbage I push his way.' *Why am I not surprised?*

'What did he have to say?'

'He feels that there is no market for a "Madrasi book". He doesn't get it. He's on this trip of publishing engineering-college love stories.'

'Well, send it along, then. Give me a week or two to get back to you.'

'Thanks, man! I promise you'll like this one.'

I sat on the balcony and smoked for a while, thinking about the months gone by, our successes and challenges, the pain-in-the-ass Jaidev Roy and, most of all, my Zorah. I got a call from Jagan.

'Sir-ji, namaskar!'

'Hello, Jagan…'

'Suryakantji wants to meet you tomorrow. He wants to review the book. Should I send the car?'

'Yes, I think sometime after 3 is okay.' I turned around to see Zorah sitting up and yawning.

'Morning! Toast and orange juice for you, my love?' She looked at me sleepy-eyed and nodded. A few minutes later, she stood behind me, with an arm wrapped around my waist, as I prepared breakfast for both of us.

Day 267

$\mathcal{I}$ pored over the newspaper, staring at the bestseller list in the *Daily Post India*. Vinod Dutta's *Bottled Up* was still scorching the charts at #1 on the bestseller list for non-fiction. Roshan's book held on at #4 and continued to ruffle feathers and form part of the chatter among the glitterati. *Jarez Rio 2030*, on the other hand, had rose from #19 to #12 in the previous fortnight, thanks to Roshan's announcement about adapting the book into a film. Even *Twilight* made an entry on the list at #21, thanks to Rohit's efforts. He had introduced a new paperback version that was bundled at a low price with *Bottled Up* and *Jarez Rio 2030*.

Sudhir entered my cabin, for once having come in based on my request, and greeted me with his cocky smile. The little success and attention over the past few weeks seemed to have got to his head, as the sales numbers for his book were now inching close to 15,000.

'Yeah, so what's up, Akshay? I have an interview with an online magazine in an hour.'

'Sales are stagnant for *Jarez Rio 2030*. We are sitting on a stockpile of over 10,000 copies that's nearly half of what we printed. Retailers are saying enough, and they claim that the numbers are slow.'

'I think the book is doing very well,' he scoffed, with little interest.

'The reviews by bloggers are also mostly negative. I told you about the climax, it isn't what it should have been…'

'Most of these guys are failed writers who are rambling away.'

'I don't believe so, many of them have a credible following. Some are successful writers themselves. We are publishing a book by one of these guys next year.'

'Why are they writing crap about my book then? Who is this writer who blogs? You could have asked him for a positive review,' he said, looking offended.

'You know I have more integrity than that.' I looked offended myself. 'Anyway, you asked us to go ahead with 25,000 copies, promising to pick up the remaining if there were any. Here's where you'll have to keep your end of the deal.'

'You want me to clear out 10,000 copies?' He looked stunned and the previous arrogance was gone.

'We don't have room for this much stock. We have *Bottled Up*'s reprint and we have a new book, Behind Closed Doors, in a week.' Zorah walked in and took a seat next to Sudhir.

'I couldn't pick up so many copies in one go. Where will I keep them? I've already picked up some 4,000 copies, most of these still remain in my beach house.'

'The market for a sci-fi fantasy isn't that much. We told you so, Sudhir,' Zorah said sharply. 'Now we're blocking up our funds and we may have to delay Anya's launch for a week.' *Boy, this girl is good.*

'Well, Sudhir, you'll have to pick up 4,000 copies at least for now,' I said, trying to sound as sympathetic as I could.

'But come on, that's a risk you have to take. That's the business you're in,' Sudhir grinned.

'Well then, I should tell Roshan Khan to call off the film. I can tell him that the book is not moving and people haven't liked it.' *Yes, I'm a pig now, wrestling with the other pigs in the mud.*

'No no, I will have 4,000 copies moved by the weekend. Please don't tell him anything,' he sweated.

'The rest will have to be taken in three to four months, if there's no movement of stock. Maybe even more, if returns come back,' Zorah said.

'No, I don't want returns to come back. Please give me some solutions, guys,' he said. I sensed desperation in his tone.

'Put out advertisements and posters in bookstores. Bundle this with Roshan's book, which means we'll need to discount the book further, lowering your royalty,' I said.

'Yes, yes…we can do that.'

'I think you should throw a success party, where you should unveil a poster for a sequel. The perception of a big success should help,' Zorah said.

'Yes, no problem! I don't mind if you discount the book much further; I don't need the royalty,' he said, before he wiped his sweaty brow and left my office.

I went back to reviewing manuscripts, particularly enjoying the book that Rahul had sent me. It was rare to see a book packed with so much of mindless slapstick humour, and had me spilling my guts out, laughing till it hurt.

Roshan Khan called, 'AK, the big man. How are you, buddy? I haven't seen you for days.' *Yes, I've had a pleasant few days not having to sit through your coke-induced bullshit!*

'Khan, yes, we should catch up, man. You're the busy one with all the films.' He was lonely these days, with many of his friends jumping ship to Rahim Khan's camp. They were seen partying with him and making appearances on his chat show, while Roshan Khan snorted coke, sulked and shot for his self-indulgent romantic film with a newcomer bimbo he seemed to be currently besotted with.

'Anyway, I was at this bookstore and I saw the posters for Anya Malik's book. Boy, she's smouldering!'

'She's a lovely girl, very talented.'

'Oh, come on, I know you guys have something going on. I've seen it in her eyes for you. Are you sleeping with her these days?'

'Of course not! You know I'm with Zorah...'

'Oh, come on! I'm married but that doesn't stop me...' *Here we go again!*

'There's nothing like that Khan. She's attractive but she's a nice kid.'

'Maybe there should be, if you want to promote your book well.' *This man has two addictions—coke and what the papers say.*

'Don't know what you mean. I got to run, Khan,' I said, before hanging up. I was scheduled to do an interview with a young reporter, Anita Joshi, of *Mumbai Gazzette*, who wanted to profile the rise of Kalim over the past year.

A petite girl, dressed down for the interview and with a very business-like demeanor entered the cabin. No sooner had we begun, than Jaidev Roy called me. I tried to ignore his calls but he kept calling.

'Just a moment, I need to take this one,' I said. 'Mr Roy, I'll talk to you a little later.'

'It's a little important, Mr Akshay. I've been reading about your new book, *Behind Closed Doors.*'

'Can we do this later? I'm in the middle of something.'

'Let's do this now. One of the stories is about this army man's wife's torrid affair with a struggling writer, isn't it? It happens in Kasauli …'

'Let's stop pussy-footing around the issue, shall we?'

'Well, Vinod Dutta had a friend from the army who lived in Kasauli. And strangely, there's a picture in Facebook, one from last year, where Anya Malik appears to have visited a village that Vinod Dutta has so eloquently written about.'

'Can we come to the point?'

'I want the translation rights to all these books, do you get it? An agreement that gives us the right to translate everything you publish into Hindi, Tamil and every other Indian language, with no questions asked.' *Ah, the damn snake.*

'Let's meet and talk.'

'I go on Gaurav Bedi's show in a week.'

'We'll meet this Saturday; why don't you come over to my office? I hear that you're in Mumbai these days.'

'Yes, I can do that,' he grunted, sounding victorious. I hung up, looking annoyed and confused about the whole episode. Quite obviously, being blackmailed wasn't something that I was used to.

'Sorry, I don't mean to pry, but was that Jaidev Roy?' Anita asked, putting down her notebook and closing the cap of her pen.

'Yeah, not one of my favourite people.'

'I'm not surprised. The man is a slimy bastard,' she said, with pent-up angst. She went from looking like a demure journalist to breathing fire like an angry tigress.

'What did he do to you?' *Boy, she looks upset.*

Tears ran down her cheeks; she took her gaze away from mine, hesitated for a moment and began.

Day 272

Jaidev Roy, dressed in a cheap khaki suit, grinned from ear to ear as he walked into my cabin, his chest swollen with pride and a haughty air about him. He exchanged angry glances with Rohit, his former employee, whom he regarded with a scornful nod.

'You finally made the right decision—why make enemies when we can work together?' he said with an air of superiority.

'Actually, the reason I called you in was to discuss a sensitive matter that's come to my attention.'

'What is that?' He looked annoyed but grinned contemptuously.

'We've recently appointed a new editor, Anita; she used to work at the *Bombay Gazette*.'

'So? What does that have to do with me?' *He looked startled at the mention of her name but bluffed quickly.*

'I understand you met her in Kolkata last year, at a literature festival...'

'I met a lot of people,' he said, feigning boredom.

'Well, this young journalist who came up to you with her manuscript was groped by you. It shocks me that you asked her to come up to your room...'

'I didn't touch her. What nonsense! I don't know what you're trying to pull off!' he screamed. He shifted uncomfortably in his chair and looked around nervously.

'Well, maybe she can go ahead and press charges then. She was threatened later too. You sent her a text that you would end her career at the newspaper.'

'Look, why are you doing this? Anyone can accuse an innocent man of these things.'

'It might be interesting for you to defend these allegations on your friend Gaurav Bedi's show.'

'Nothing like this happened! The girl is talking rubbish and you're trying to frame me!' His eyes were bloodshot and he spat his words out, looking like a diseased mongrel.

'Fine, let's fight it out then. Let her go to the cops and the media. We'll let this play out, shall we?'

'No, don't! What do you want from me?' *I love this game of chess.*

'A clean slate, for one! You maintain your silence and maybe I can persuade her to put aside these serious allegations...'

'Done,' he said with desperation before he got up to leave.

'There's another. You'll apologize to her in person. She isn't here today but I'll set a date and time.'

'I could do that. I was really drunk and made a mistake,' he said, looking away painfully.

'It's shameful, man,' I said, to which he averted his gaze, before lifting himself out of the chair and leaving my cabin.

Anita walked in a short while later. 'What did he say?'

'He was indignant at first but now he is quite scared! You should have seen his face; it turned white like a sheet.'

'He wouldn't even remember if it happened. He was pissed

drunk when he asked me up to his room,' she said.

'Yeah, I'm going to set up a meeting tomorrow. Let him come and apologize for what he did.'

'Oh, I don't know...you think that's necessary? It was a while ago,' she said, looking concerned.

'He may be the biggest in the business but that's the least he can do. He's got to respect you and, yeah, it is necessary.'

Two days later, a pale-faced Jaidev Roy, looking five years older than his normal self, turned up on Gaurav Bedi's show to talk about the phenomenal rise of his publishing firm and their plans. Bedi, with his deep baritone and "I'm educated, you're not" air of superiority, cheekily enough brought my name into the conversation.

'So, what is your opinion of this upstart from London, Akshay Mathur? He seems to think that Indian writers are country bumpkins from the boondocks.' He smiled like a smelly old coot at Jaidev Roy, who gritted his teeth and looked like he'd been given an electric shock.

'Er...no, I don't hold that view. I think he's brought a lot of fresh writing into the market. We have a lot to learn from him,' Jaidev said calmly.

'Oh, what has he done, apart from sing and dance with has-beens and other nasty people from Bollywood?' *Looks like the old bastard's BP is on a rise.*

'Probably a lot more than many literature enthusiasts have done for the lot of writers in this country,' Jaidev said, fixing his steely gaze at the old fox, who looked crushed, and decided to move on and go for a commercial break. Zorah and I were in splits watching this fiasco, and it seemed like Jaidev Roy, who was gunning for our throats, was now becoming a staunch supporter of Kalim.

The same evening, we made an appearance at Sudhir's success party at Zenzi. The place was packed with familiar faces who had turned up at every other party, and Zorah moved aside to bond with journalists and friends in the media. Seema Patel, the wife of a famous restaurateur, walked up to me.

'You are really pulling the punches, I tell you,' she said, showing of her pearly white implants.

'Oh thanks, we just got lucky with some interesting books.' *We made some interesting and, yeah, swapped an author here and there.*

'I'm so amazed and so impressed,' she said, nodding like a schoolteacher and sipping on her wine.

'Thank you.'

'I wanted to ask you something. May I?'

'Indeed, go ahead.'

'I want to start a vanity publishing imprint. You know, something that aims at co-publishing with celebrities for their biographies and memoirs. I know so many people who are keen to have a book out…' *Interesting!*

'Of course, it's a great opportunity. I see a lot of it happening in the UK. And here, it will take someone like you, who is well connected, to make it happen.'

'Oh, wonderful!' she gushed, going from schoolteacher to a 17-year-old. 'So will you partner with us?'

'Sorry, what's that again?'

'You know, I could find and choose the books. You can get your team to edit, sell and market. Your events and marketing efforts are spot on.'

'It sounds interesting; let me pitch it to Angus and I'll call you soon,' I said. I promised to work on a plan with her and moved to the bar to get a drink.

Another gentleman who looked like he'd come from a business meeting accosted me. 'Naresh Shah,' he said, pumping my hand. He was old and morose, and had an air of intellectual arrogance about him.

'Nice to meet you,' I said, trying to move away to Anya, who looked bored, with Sudhir sticking to her like a leech. She noticed me standing on the other side and made eyes at me.

'You are a publisher, aren't you? I've authored 12 books. Many of them have been very successful. You must have heard of *I'm the Boss* and *Office Psychopath*. Those were written by me.'

'That's wonderful!' I said, as I tried to sidle away. 'You see, I've written this new book about corporate–political conspiracies. It's about how five industrialists are running this country through puppet politicians.'

'Really?'

He looked around carefully to make sure that the CID wasn't watching us. 'It's the truth. I've done a lot of research and gathered a lot of evidence,' he whispered. *Oh, a conspiracy theory, is it?*

'Oh, that's amazing.' *This guy's a riot.*

'Yes, here's my card. I'm a management advisor. I'm on the board of many companies. I also lecture at all the leading business schools. You can see my website; it has many wonderful inspirational quotes, all written by me.' His designation said 'Founder, Partner, Management Motivator and Chief Management Advisor'. On the reverse, it had a ghastly picture of him showing off his teeth. *What a quack!*

'I could use some inspiration,' I said, egging him on.

'Wonderful! Maybe you can publish another book as well. One with all my management quotes and tips for a happy corporate life,' he grinned like a madman. *Yeah, we could call it 'The Diary Of a Corporate Quack'.*

'I'll call you,' I said, moving closer to Zorah, who took my arm and introduced me to a few journalists.

'What were you talking about with Naresh Shah?'

'You know him?'

'Yeah, he was the former CEO of a bank which collapsed years ago. The government had to step in and sell it to another bank. He's a whacko! Imagine, he was decorating his office and launching a book on mantras of corporate success while business at the bank torpedoed.'

'Yes, he's one strange old geezer.'

'He goes around as a briefcase professor to some third-rate management schools. I don't know who invited him here,' she said with a laugh.

'Beats me!' *Boy, what a character.* We left a few minutes later, after briefly chatting with Anya about her upcoming launch. The posters, shot with her on the cover, were making waves, and the book had become a much-anticipated release, with over 10,000 advance copies being ordered.

Later that night, I received a called from Angus, who had warmed up to me considerably of late.

'So mate, I was talking to dad the other night and he's quite excited about the proposal of doing a literary e-books imprint.'

'He is?'

'Yeah mate. He's mighty impressed with the work you're doing back in India. We've been discussing with a number of parties who want to buy Kalim of us.'

'I don't know, Angus, I think you should wait out a bit. India offers way more potential than England right now, and you wouldn't want to sell a business that's starting to find its feet in the market.'

'Umm yeah, I agree. But we want you out here to lead the new project. If we do decide to stay in India with Kalim, he just wants you to stay around for a few months and help transition Kalim to a new leadership. So let's begin that process, eh?'

'Yeah, well, sticking with Kalim is the best thing you can do. Give me some time, mate, let me think a bit more about coming back to London.'

'Are you changing your mind?'

'No, it's just that I feel like I have unfinished business here. Like I need to finish some of the things I've set in motion. I feel like I am responsible for these books…'

'Seems like Zorah is holding you back, eh? You're in love with her, aren't you?' *I guess I am.*

'I don't think that's what it is. Let's talk about moving back after a month. Moreover, don't sell Kalim. It'll be the worst mistake of your life.' I hung up and spent the evening reading short stories by Sankar and Premchand, immersed deeply in the world they'd created through their writing, which I hoped would be popular for centuries to come.

Day 291

The launch of Anya's *Behind Closed Doors* turned out to be a massive success. We had worked up a storm with pictures of her from the shoot being posted by her on Twitter, excerpts from the book printed in a leading national magazine and even managing to get Anya to don the covers of two fashion magazines. The bookstore was packed with a young audience of twenty-somethings and, quite clearly, we had preached to the choir with this one. The store manager, never having seen such crowds for a no-celebrity launch, had to call for extra chairs and push bookshelves out of the way to make way for the audience. Anya played the glamorous diva to the hilt, flapping her eyelids, giggling and posing for the shutterbugs in her designer dress. This was her moment, something to make up for scraping her futuristic love story, and she wasn't letting it go to waste. She made a splash in the papers the next day with pictures from the launch, a mention of the event's success and glowing reviews for the book, which was described as 'fresh', 'breathtaking', 'sensual and epic treatment of emotions' and 'surreal'.

Even the old fogey Gaurav Bedi was arm-twisted into inviting her to his flagging talk show and gush eloquently about how beautiful she was and how much he loved the book. Sudhir, meanwhile, sulked about how the publicity on his book was much weaker and that we had failed to offer him as much support. He began to complain about *Jarez Rio 2030* being relegated to the back shelves and *Behind Closed Doors* dominating every inch of space possible in the new releases list across bookstores. In an attempt to placate him, Zorah decided to help host a launch event in Chennai and Bengaluru, where his book was doing better than in most other cities. She flew down with him for the event, while I was busy talking to newspapers on our recent successes and editing our next two releases.

Roshan Khan called me out of the blue to discuss my plans for the weekend.

'I plan to relax. Zorah should be back on Monday,' I said. *I hope to not see your face or watch you getting stoned and cry about how messed up your love life is.*

'Nah nah, that's why I called. I'm hosting a success party for Anya on Saturday night. I'll see you at Prive,' he said, before hanging up.

'Sure.' *Oh, shoot!* Anya called moments later and made elaborate plans about going together to the party, describing it as a great photo opportunity. Roshan, now hobnobbing with writers instead of the mostly filmy crowd, got coverage into the papers about the upcoming party for his 'sweetest friend', Anya. It turned out to be a hilarious feature that could have provoked Gaurav Bedi to consider suicide. 'I no longer represent just Bollywood; I'm a writer too. Those from the literary circle are my people too,' he quoted with his cheesy smile and posing with a picture of his book. He also added, 'It was on my insistence that Akshay agreed to publish such a bold and provocative collection, as I saw the spark of talent in Anya.' Reading it on my iPad at Anya's apartment almost made me throw up my lunch. After cursing Roshan under my breath, I reached for a cold beer and then another while Anya took her time getting ready for her big night.

Once the night approached, and with Zorah away, I made an entrance with Anya. She wore a short, red dress and clung to my arm as she smiled and posed for the photographers. As Roshan Khan, who had managed to colour-coordinate with her, wearing a suit and a maroon shirt, stuck close to Anya, I moved quietly towards the bar. I could drink without inhibition tonight. I was tired of talking to journalists and repeating why we were successful, and so sick and tired of the people I was forced to rub shoulders with at these parties. I noticed Anish Kumar, a failed actor from the '90s, chat up a young starlet while putting his arm slowly around her waist. Not far from him, his cosmetic surgery-loving wife showing her cleavage in a revealing dress, enjoying an intimate conversation with Surjeet Jha, a struggling actor, who made rounds of the parties and followed Roshan Khan around. I ducked and hid behind one of the waiters, as I saw Naresh Shah walking towards the bar looking for me. A moment later, Roshan Khan's staff rudely intercepted him. I overheard a heated argument, where he was accused of 'gatecrashing'. He claimed to have been Roshan's banker for years, and after a brief exchange of words, he turned around, his face flushed pink, and walked away with a huff. *Such are the ways of this world!* I finished three beers in quick succession and was thinking of an excuse to get out of there, when Anya walked up with a smile on her face.

'Why are you looking so bored?' she asked with her flirty smile. I noticed eyes in the room fix their gaze on us and it appeared like we were having an intimate conversation.

'I'm quite tired of this bullshit! I need a break... All this publicity... makes me feel like a showpiece,' I said, before picking up another drink.

'You know, it's the same for me,' she said softly, resting her head on my shoulders and then slowing leaning in, with her hot breath in my face and her intoxicating fragrance messing with my head. I got to know what happened next in the newspapers the next morning.

'Roshan Khan throws a wild bash for Anya', the Page 3 headlines said. Half the pictures were of Anya and me at different points of time during the party. Each had a different caption. A picture of Anya and me entering the party was captioned: Akshay and Anya—the literary power couple. One with both of us and Roshan Khan was captioned: the lovebirds and their BFF. Another, when she had rested her head on my chest at the bar, had the description: Anya and her pillar of support. Finally, there was one of both of us leaving the party, me looking smashed and she looking satisfied. This one read: 'Akshay was earlier seeing Zorah, the daughter of the late owner of Kalim, a firm he now presides over.' *Oh, this is dangerous bullshit! What exactly happened last night?*

I sat up. I was still wearing my clothes from the party, and Anya came out of the restroom. 'Good morning,' she said cheerfully. 'You guys have a nice place.' *Oh no!*

'What happened last night?' *I'm screwed.*

'The coverage is fantastic, isn't it? They're finally pairing us up together,' she winked. *Zorah is going to shred me to bits.*

'About last night, I'm sorry I was wasted... I shouldn't have...'

'Relax, nothing happened. We just kissed at the party a little

and I ended up driving you home because you were drunk.
I put you to bed and then you fell asleep. I slept on your sofa,'
she said, punching me playfully.

'We kissed at the party? Like people saw us?'

'Yeah, they took pictures too. Only *Mid-Afternoon* is printing
them, with a little bit about us necking at the party,' she said
gleefully.

'Oh man! What am I going to tell Zorah?'

'Relax, it's good publicity. Why do you think I did it?' *Ouch!*

'I thought you had this thing for me...'

'Oh come on, I have a girlfriend, Asmita—she's been
my yoga instructor for two years now. All this, the old man
turning into the author of some essays about poor people and
the environment, me turning into the author of a collection
of erotica, making out with you... It was destined to happen.
There's a purpose, you know,' she said thoughtfully.

'Which is?'

'Me getting ahead in life! I want to be the most popular
woman writer in the country. If I've had to do all this to get there,
so be it,' she said, looking like a different person. *Another vixen.*

My phone rang just then. 'How could you?' It was Zorah
at the other end, and she was sobbing.

'It isn't like what they say.' *Oh blimey!*

'There are pictures of you kissing her, Akshay!' *From AK
to Akshay, damn!*

'It's a camera angle...'

'Shut up! The journos from all the papers were there. I've
got calls telling me what happened.'

'So you believe them and not me?'

'What isn't true, Akshay? That you entered the party with

her hand in yours, that you hung around her all the time and made out with her? You even left together...' Anya stood there with a hand on her chin, looking amused.

'I don't know...I was smashed. It's a mistake...honest.'

'Look, let's get some breakfast at Out Of the Blue; you both can argue later. I'm famished,' Anya said. *Shut up, Anya!*

'She's there?' Zorah shouted.

'I can explain. Nothing happened...'

'Sure, I should have known before dating a schmuck with a drinking problem...this is where I was going to end up.'

'Come on...I don't have a problem!'

'It's over, Akshay! Please move out before I get back tomorrow...' Anya, sensing the tension, gave me a soft peck on the cheek, waved and tiptoed out of the apartment in her heels and her little number.

'It can't be; you've got to...'

'Why can't it? The papers are saying it's over already,' she said with a bitter laugh, before hanging up.

Anya came back inside. 'I don't have any money,' she said, smiling like a brat. *Shoot me...*

'Wait, I'll get dressed in a few minutes and drive you home.' *Bollocks! What the hell have I done!*

'Thanks. Let's get some coffee and have breakfast before that. I'm so hung over and fucking starved,' she said, as I stood there stunned, with an empty feeling coming over me.

Day 301

Zorah left the apartment as soon as she saw me open the door. She refused to pay heed to my pleas, my messages were not replied to and my calls went unanswered. I got a terse call from her friend, Preeti. 'Please move out of Zorah's apartment,' she said and hung up. I spent a couple of nights on Rohit's squeaky old couch, before I moved temporarily into a service apartment. It was a week since Zorah had spoken to me and the atmosphere in office was quiet and subdued. Despite the raging success of Anya's book, the fact that we had Jaidev Roy off our back and that we had new staff on board with a promising list being built up, the tension was palpable to everyone in office. It was like people expected a showdown to happen but Zorah got on with her work as usual, refusing to look at me or acknowledge me. Anything that had to come to me from her now came through Sita. These days, Sita looked at me like she wanted to bite off my neck. Even Mr Samuel shrugged his shoulders in dismay and muttered a 'hrrmph' with a grumpy look plastered on his face every time he saw me.

I, on the other hand, had to keep up appearances and had spent the past few days accompanying Anya for the launch of her book in Pune and Delhi. *Behind Closed Doors* was on top of the heap as the #1 fiction bestseller and we had the unique distinction of dominating both the fiction and the non-fiction lists. I had cemented my place as the poster boy of new-age Indian publishing. Editorials were written about how I brought market knowledge and experience from the UK and blended that with local sensibilities. The big five publishers went on a massive headhunt to replace their lazy, conceited, wine-sipping and Rushdie-loving editors with young ones from the West and some well-known scribes, who could pump some energy into the business. The Page 3 media continued to pair Anya and me together, and Roshan Khan created a flurry of sorts when he revealed that he was keen to snap up the rights to a couple of stories in Anya's collection, which she now legally held copyrights to. The press jumped into the fray, like moths to a flame. They did a feature on Anya then and now. A full-page feature appeared on her journey from a sappy teenage queen to a bold, beautiful woman. There was another piece on successful young women and their sugar daddies, and knowing my luck, I made the top of the list, with a picture of Anya and me included.

Zorah didn't show up to work the morning the article appeared. Despite repeated attempts, all I got was the recorded message—'the number you are trying is switched off'. I hoped and prayed for her forgiveness. I wanted her to yell at me, slap me and prevent me from having to do anything with Anya, but none of that happened. I spent the evenings in office, immersed in work, trying to wind up the editing of Suryakant Joshi's biography and another book. Anya turned up in her Versace dress on Sohail Malik's show the next evening. Half the time was spent on her talking about how I inspired and mentored her, and her giggling about me being 'gentle and sensitive'. *Oh, get over it!*

Soon after the show was telecast, I got a call from Roshan Khan.

'This affair with Anya Malik has gotten pretty steamy, huh, chief?' *Screw you!*

'Yes, it has to be honest. I don't understand how things got around to getting so messed up.'

'It's always complicated with the ladies' man,' he said with his fake laugh.

'I mean, I don't even fancy this woman, she isn't my type… For God's sake, she is a…' *I can't say it, I can't be like her.*

'You went and cheated on Zorah, man! That's pretty nasty!' *Didn't you encourage me to, you two-faced son of a b****?*

'It was a mistake, I was drunk.'

'Yeah, it happens to me sometimes, chief! What's the plan now?'

'I don't know… We'll chat later,' I said, before hanging up. I pondered the past few weeks and the good times with Zorah, before forcing myself to focus on work. In the young writer Sunil Kumar's book, *Auto Shankar*, I found 'the' Indian novel I had been hunting for since I started this job. It was uninhibited, with tongue-in-cheek humour; the plot was adventurous and the writing crisp and unpretentious, making it one hell of a compelling read. I signed the author on immediately and aimed to release this on the back of the success of Anya's book. Advance orders would be respectable and the stores would greet it with enthusiasm, given our track record.

Just as I was winding up with the final edits, Zorah came knocking. She looked breathtaking in her mauve top and black formal skirt, and entered my cabin quietly, fixing her piercing gaze at me, while I looked at her with trepidation.

'AK, we need to talk,' she said softly, as she bit her lip and looked a tad nervous. *Finally!*

'Zo, it was a horrible mistake…'

'Wait, AK, please let me finish.' She turned to me with steely-eyed determination.

'Sorry, please go ahead.'

'I'm leaving Kalim, AK. And no, don't look at me like that. I don't think it's possible that we can carry on working together after what has happened.'

'Listen Zo…'

'No, you listen to me, alright? I'm leaving in two months. I just want you to look for a replacement. I'll see through Sunil Kumar's and Suryakant Joshi's launches.' I looked at her with astonishment; I didn't know how to react. 'I'm going to start working with Roshan as his publicist,' she said with some hesitation, which seemed like a slap on my face.

'You'll leave Kalim to go work for him? Come on Zo, let's move on, shall we.'

'AK, I told you…' she said with tears her eyes, while I turned away and banged the table with my fist.

'Okay Zo, do what you have to, alright? What can I say?' *I'm sorry, don't go and work for that shark.*

'Thanks,' she said, recovering her composure and wiping her tears. If there was a moment that I felt gutted, crushed and completely heartbroken, this was it. I didn't feel this way when my marriage to Janice collapsed. I was glad it ended, and I was happy to move. This time that's the last thing I wanted to do.

My phone rang incessantly. I picked it up on impulse; it was a number I didn't recognize.

'Yeah?'

'Hello sir, myself Dushyant Lal from Kanpur, sir. I loved *Behind Closed Doors*. What a book!'

'Thank you. Look, you can drop your lines of appreciation for the book on our feedback page or maybe on our Facebook page…'

'Sir, actually, I am a writer. I was wondering if you will publish my book. It's a story of this young girl who ends up having sex…'

'Look buddy, please follow the guidelines on our website, yeah?'

'No, but sir, will you publish it? It has lots of sex, teenagers will like…'

'You will have to submit it first and our editorial team will see.' *1,2,3…*

'Arey, only if you will publish, I will sit and write it na?' *I see… crackhead!*

I hung up on him and went up to the terrace for a smoke and some fresh air. Zorah, while pretending to get on with her work, turned to look at me with sadness in her eyes; she was possibly wondering how I'm dealing with it.

I went up and pondered her decision. I was irate with that snake, Roshan Khan, who grabbed this opportunity to offer her a job. I decided to take off for a week or two and go down to Goa, a place I'd last visited with my ex-wife, who was then my girlfriend.

I spoke to Rohit and Anita briefly about the launch of Sunil Kumar's book and asked them to brief Zorah as well. I left the three of them a long email of things to do and, after putting Rohit in charge of the office, I walked out of the building before sunset for the first time in a long time. I deserved a break from this madness, and it was about time I took it.

Three hours later, I packed up and left for the airport, ignoring Anya's message—'Do you want to party with Asmita and me tonight?'—and Roshan's—'Are you okay, buddy?'

Angus called later that night and asked if I was ready to move back to London in a couple of months to get the literary imprint started. I said, 'Yes, I'd very much like to come back home.'

Day 312

After 10 days of sitting on the beach in Goa and ruing my fuck-ups in the recent past, I was back at work, much to the relief of Rohit, who was battling calls from Anya, Sudhir and even Jagan, who was chasing up on Suryakant Joshi's book. I was relatively in a better frame of mind post the long break. I entered office and bumped into Zorah, she of the luscious lips and hips that swayed like a response to sweet jazz music. She almost blurted out a hello, before she decided that she was mad at me and walked away.

I called in a meeting with the whole team, followed up on progress in the past couple of weeks and broke the news of Zorah deciding to leave the firm post the launch of Suryakant Joshi's book. I said that there wasn't the need for her to leave, as this was her home, and that she needed to lead this firm to bigger successes. The reaction was a muted response: Rohit looked tired, Mr Samuel was his grumpy self, Anita looked sorry, Sita seemed really upset and made a clicking sound with her throat, and Zorah, with tears welling up, turned away and stared stoically at the floor. I slipped in the fact that I'm moving back to London in the coming months, soon after we have on board a new commissioning editor.

'So, I hope in two months, I'll be the one who's gone and Zorah will still be here as your new CEO. It's what Angus and I both want.' Zorah's gaze locked with mine but she restrained from saying anything in response. 'Everyone, we need to make Sunil Kumar's book, *Auto Shankar*, a big success. It's our most credible effort. To be honest, it will be our biggest test, as it's an unknown author without marketing muscle or PR machinery behind him.' This seemed to cheer them up a little; it gave them a sense of purpose.

'I just want to say that each of you is incredible at what you do. Thanks for your support,' I said, betraying more emotion than I'd done in the past, which softened the mood a bit and managed to get me a pat on my back from Mr Samuel before he went back to his favourite hobby of scanning the tabloid on who's screwing who and what people are wearing to parties and events.

Speaking of which, the previous day's paper carried the image of Zorah leaving a musician friend's party with Roshan Khan. There was also a comment about how his wife and he were separating and how he'd been seen recently with young starlets, and now Zorah Kalim. The news made me sick till the pit of my stomach and I turned the pages to see Anya's *Behind Closed Doors* on top of the bestseller lists; even *Jarez Rio 2030* clung on to a position of #20 on the list. I had to ensure one more success in order to meet the challenge that Angus posed before us.

In the days that followed, we launched *Auto Shankar* with a subtle media campaign. It was a subdued launch at a sub-urban bookstore, where Anya Malik, who looked her pretty self and pouted for pictures by clinging on to my arm, flanked the author, and Sudhir, who sulked a bit, spoke more about his own book and its perceived success than about the book being launched. At leading bookstores across the country, we had posters of the book cover, designed by a talented young student whom Zorah had commissioned the work to. Slowly but surely, in the week that followed, praise and support for the book flowed in. Unlike Sudhir's PR-managed moderate success or Anya's glamour quotient and risqué content of *Behind Closed Doors*, this lighthearted tale of an autorickshaw-driver-turned-superhero won the hearts of thousands of youngsters, who read the book, blogged about it and tweeted their support for the young writer. The result was a more-than-anticipated demand for the book. No sooner had glowing reviews appeared, than Sunil Kumar was toasted as the next big thing. We began to receive calls from producers who were queuing up to snap up the adaptation rights. Rahim Khan's older brother, Rashid, walked into my office one morning and made an offer for the rights that neither Sunil nor I could turn down.

Auto Shankar, starring Rahim Khan, was pitted to take on the adaptation of one of Anya's stories from *Behind Closed Doors,* being adapted into a feature by Roshan, who seemed to be becoming close with Anya and included her in his inner circle. Meanwhile, *Auto Shankar's* sales soared with all the publicity and hype, given Rahim's own following, which was less PR-oriented and more driven by his own fans, who couldn't get enough of his bravado and bad-boy act. Roshan reacted with his typical style, feeling insecure and betrayed, like a 12 year-old. He planted stories about me cozying up to Rahim Khan after I'd been reprimanded by him for cheating on Zorah. What followed was a heated altercation between us at a party in Olive, after which he stopped calling me. The vibes from his camp were negative, with planted stories again of how I'd thrown a drunken fit at the party and picked up a fight with the great actor who made things happen for me in the city. Zorah stayed out of the battle and seemed annoyed with the undue publicity.

I strolled into work late, having partied with Rahim Khan and his boys the previous night, and heady with the recent success of *Auto Shankar*, which invoked kind words from a grumbling Gaurav Bedi. As I was settling down to oversee Anita's work on Shweta Iyer's manuscript and finalize bits and ends on Suryakant Joshi's book, I heard a commotion in office. I walked out of my cabin to see three overweight policemen talking to Mr Samuel, who appeared tense with their presence. Sita looked shocked, Zorah looked pale, and Rohit and Anita stood by looking confused as I stepped out.

'Can I help you, officers?' I asked, sporting a grin and trying to ease the tension. Rohit, Anita and Zorah moved closer and stood behind me.

'*Toh aap hain* Akshay Sharma?' the senior among them, with a salt and pepper moustache asked, while the sweaty ones stood behind him and regarded me with a grimace.

One of them stepped forward and pointed at me, '*Yes sir, yahi hai. Bollywood ke connections hain iske. Saari raat woh Roshan Khan ke saath night club mein…*'

'That would be me. What seems to be the problem?' *Did I get into a fight last night?*

'You need to come with us. There are some investigations on what has been going on in this office,' he said, with an air of suspicion.

'We just publish books from this office, nothing that shouldn't be done or is against the law, but what is the problem?'

'*Suryakant Joshi se connection hai? Koi kitaab chhap rahi hai?*'

'I've helped him…but what is this about?' I asked, looking confused.

'You have to come with me, Akshay Sharma. We are taking you with us for questioning,' the big man said. Zorah, on an impulse, pressed her hand into mine.

'*Pooch taach*,' the one with paan-stained teeth said. *Fuck me, what is this now? I'm being hauled away!*

'I think I want to call a lawyer,' I said, trying to look calm and composed, while Sita stood there with her mouth open and everyone else looked scared.

'Not necessary, we aren't arresting you. Only routine questioning, please cooperate,' he said, raising his voice.

'Well…let's go then,' I said with a forced smile, as one of the cops moved in behind me almost on cue. Mr Samuel looked like he'd seen it all.

'Where are you taking him? This isn't right. You can't take him away…what has he done?' Zorah said, stepping up and screaming in the officer's face.

'Madam, please don't interfere in police work,' he said with calm force.

'I will bring the media to the police station. You can't…'

'You'll be putting his life in danger,' the boss said defiantly, before whisking me away. A harrowed Zorah, with Anita and Rohit in tow, followed us down. We walked past the shops and other enterprises downstairs, with me feeling like a bank robber.

'Don't worry,' I said weakly to Zorah, before the Tata Sumo drove away.

Instead of the police station, I was taken to a private bungalow and ushered into a large, opulent living room. A portly man in a khaki waistcoat and a white kurta entered the room, followed by three tough-looking guys in navy blue safari suits. *Wait a minute, it's the Chief Minister.*

'Sit down, Akshay,' he said, like he was referring to a long-lost friend. 'We met at Roshan Khan's cousin's wedding,' he added. *Roshan is using the CM to warn me? Dude!*

'I remember. But why am I here, sir? Am I in some kind of trouble?'

'Yes and no,' he said, before scratching his oily hair and stroking the edges of his kurta. 'You're writing some book for Suryakant Joshi, right?'

I nodded along and shook my head, wondering what I had got myself into. 'There's been a lot of chatter about it. One of my confidants picked up something from a party, where someone was referring to some big revelations coming in the book.'

'I haven't revealed anything about the book, sir.'

'I know, it's someone else and we've taken care of it.' He looked composed and sported his toothy smile. 'The party president has requested me to talk to you.'

'Hmm...' *Go on.*

'You see, we hear that the book has some interesting information about our political opponent. Our party president is very interested in getting more information. We can cooperate,' he said with a conspiratorial smile. 'You see, elections are in two months...' *And you're bidding for your bosses.*

'It would be unethical to part with the manuscript without Suryakant Joshi's...'

'You see, with the government on your side, you have full

protection. We just arrested four rowdies yesterday who had been contracted to beat you up.' *What?*

If this affected me, I didn't show it.

'The opposition are rabble-rousers. They are likely to send in their activists to create riots and disturbance. We have to protect public property and maintain law and order. In the interest of this, I request you to hand in this book.'

'Alright, but I want my staff and myself to be fully protected.'

'You already are. You have an undercover force from the Home Ministry watching your office and your homes. No one can touch you,' he said, like a man in control.

'Much appreciate that…' *This sounds like being in a James Bond film.*

'Now let's have lunch and Pandey will escort you back to your office. That *Auto Shankar* book was really funny…too good!' he grinned. *Whew!*

I walked into office three hours later. I messed up my hair, loosened my tie and unbuttoned my shirt for the effect. 'You're back,' Zorah shrieked. Everyone looked at me with surprise, anxiety and relief. They were all standing huddled around Zorah, who looked like she'd been crying. Watching me enter, she ran across the room and leapt into my arms. She kissed my cheek and pressed her face into my chest, 'I'm sorry,' she whispered. *Mmm…I love the smell of this hair and the warmth of this body.* 'I was so worried…'

'I'm sorry, love. Don't worry, everything is alright, I'm okay,' I said, turning to the rest of the group, with my arm firmly around Zorah's waist. They'd watched us with curiosity and with a relieved smile.

'Nothing, guys, the CM was wondering what Suryakant

Joshi's book was about and asked me to join him for lunch. I need a nap, it was heavy...' I said with a smirk, to which the rest of them laughed.

'That's what this was about?' *It seems to have saved my life.*
Ah-huh
'Ah-huh.'

'You had me so worried, I cried so much,' she said, whacking my arm as we entered my cabin. *A nice turnaround of affairs, ain't it?*

'You're my sweet little drama queen, aren't you?' She smiled dreamily and hugged me again. *And one heck of an angry woman!*

'Let's leave early, you're coming back home with me,' she hissed.

'Yeah, for sure.'

Day 331

*I*t's the morning of the launch of Suryakant Joshi's autobiography that has created a political storm. What happened before that, you ask?

Well, soon after meeting my friend the Chief Minister, I moved back home, back to our cozy little apartment and in the arms of the craziest, most jealous and most beautiful and loving woman I know.

'It's like a dream...us getting back together,' I said, cuddling her after the best sex we had ever had.

'Why? You give up hope too easily,' she said, touching my cheek playfully and intertwining her legs with mine under the sheets.

'You threw me out of the apartment and stopped talking to me.'

'Baba, I was angry, na!' she said, making a baby face. 'But I expected you to do some drama; maybe sing under my balcony, got drunk and come knocking in the middle of the night, or maybe even requested a song on the radio... But you just sulked...'

'Jeez, what was I supposed to do? I thought you'd get mad

at me if I did any of that…'

'No, I would have loved it,' she cooed. *Girls! Go figure…*

'So you weren't that mad at me, after all?'

She grinned and played with my hair. 'I was, about you getting drunk like that…but you mustn't forget I have friends in the media. I got to know that Anya was throwing herself at you and that Roshan had those stories planted about both of you.' *Oh, that serpent!*

'What? I'm going to get that son of a…'

'He's been hitting on me since the day the stories made the press. Now that his wife has left him…'

'But you were to join him, weren't you?'

Her face wore an impish grin, while I lay there looking confused. 'Was I? That's what I told you, just for kicks. I also accompanied him to a party and skipped out a few minutes into it.'

'You're mean. I took this nice little break in Goa. On the flight back, I'm hit with these pictures in the tabloid.'

'Ha ha…well, it gives you some sense of how I felt, sweetie.'

'I'm sorry! You know she didn't even like me, after all. She was doing this for publicity and kicks.'

'I know. She called me the same morning after you said that you were leaving and wanted me to stay on. She explained everything and apologized.'

'You knew?' *Seems like the joke was on me all this while.*

'Yes, baba! I did, but I was confused and didn't know how to react or to tell you not to leave. Do you know what went down in Bengaluru?'

'What?'

'You'll love this. Sudhir showed me the coverage in the

tabloids at breakfast in the hotel. Five minutes later, after I've sobbed before him, he goes down on his knees and asks me to marry him…' she said, looking bemused.

'That weasel…' *I'm going to burn his books!*

'It was embarrassing, but hilarious as well. He took that single stem from the little vase on the table. I literally walked out on him,' she giggled.

'Attagirl.' *If that isn't one opportunist bastard!*

'Yeah, and in the hotel later, I completely had a go at him. Told him to go bury himself. Haven't heard from him since. We took separate seats on the flight back.'

'That's funny,' I said, before turning to grab the remote and turn on the breakfast news.

Now back to Suryakant Joshi's tell-all. The leader of opposition, Madan Gokhle, was screaming 'it's not true. It's a conspiracy by the government,' in chaste Hindi before television cameras, which captured an unflattering pose of his scratching his bald head and rubbing his protruding belly with a constipated look on his face. What unravelled was a political scandal blowing up in the face of the seasoned politician. The authorities had selectively leaked excerpts from the book to leading national magazines and newspapers, which now had a new cover story: 'Madan Gokhle's love affair revealed: What makes Madan Gokhle so hateful.' The Chief Minister fired a masterstroke: 'He is scarred by his past. He shouldn't vent out his hatred against other communities. I'm a firm believer in karma.' This led to his flagging rating to shoot up, while Madan Gokhle's poll ratings went in free fall. Over the next few days, OB Vans showed up in his village and interviewed the woman in question, who was now a poor widow. Heads and state chiefs distanced themselves from Madan Gokhle. 'We have never declared Madan Gokhleji as the chief ministerial candidate. He is, of course, a tall figure but the party will be led by the young generation,' said the party president, R.V. Guru Reddy, pointing at the nervous 65-year-olds sitting behind him with a grim expression. Madan Gokhle, was, however, defiant and 'refused to give up' while 'denying all charges' and describing the book as a way of 'settling old scores'.

Suryakant Joshi, the wily politician, who was closely in touch with the present government, went AWOL and surfaced two days before the launch, where he defiantly claimed that everything in the book was true and challenged Madan Gokhle to prove him wrong. A small group of Apna Democratic Party activists who showed up outside our office were quickly dispelled with lathis and a few kicks on their behinds from the harrowed policemen who stood guard outside, braving the heat and humidity. Zorah and I, meanwhile, were on television every day, in conversation with leading anchors and debating the subject of controversy with politicians and other political observers. The Chief Minister was happy, as it won him some brownie points from his bosses and put the embarrassed opposition on the back foot. He decided to show up at the launch and unveil the book with Suryakant Joshi. The advance orders for the book were unprecedented. Angus called in with orders of 20,000 copies each for the US and UK markets, while bookstores cleared a whole rack to stack the book. Orders were taken online a month in advance and the book was a #1 bestseller before anyone had even read it.

The launch, after many tense moments, which involved security clearances, change of venues and a number of media briefings, turned out to be an affair attended just by national media and a select list of people. Suryakant Joshi went about things calmly, kicking things off with reciting Rabindranath Tagore and Kabir's *dohas*. He spoke briefly about his childhood, the importance of education, and his success and failures as a minister. He went on to field a limited set of questions that were cleared beforehand about Madan Gokhle and signed off with the words, 'It's sad that his political career had to end like this. He could have shown more compassion and done better as a human being while occupying the seats of power.' The flashbulbs went off and the portly Chief Minister grinned like a kid who had been handed candy.

The next morning, Madan Gokhle withdrew his nomination for election citing health reasons. He also wryly admitted to knowing the woman in question and having a childhood crush on her. He stood baffled before the cameras, having aged by 10 years in the past two weeks, and apologized to the nation for 'indiscretions towards certain communities while in office'.

A charged-up Central Government ordered a full CBI inquiry into the matter, and jubilant ministers and celebrities seeking attention tweeted their own opinion on the matter, which in other words was no different than calling Madan Gokhle 'vindictive' and condoning his acts as 'shameful'. The Opposition, which pulled his face off the posters and seemed crushed by the revelations, quietly sidelined him. Our phones never stopped ringing with congratulatory messages, and others seeking favours, taking the opportunity to praise our 'guts' in publishing such a path-breaking book. A couple of threatening calls were swiftly dealt with by the police, with one turning out to be an Apna Democratic Party rabble-rouser and the other a drunk kid who wanted to mess with my head for rejecting his epic. We also ended up receiving a few calls from a former political secretary in the south and another in Delhi, who wanted to write tell-all exposés on scams and past events that they'd witnessed.

After a well-attended and publicized party at his farmhouse, Suryakant Joshi, along with his family, retreated to Shimla, where he was to cool his heels for the next five years as the new Governor of Himachal Pradesh—an appointment made hastily by the current government, which he had found favour with and which didn't want to see his political ambitions grow bigger than a relaxed role in the hills. 'Both of you please do come and stay with us. I would very much like that,' he told Zorah and me the day before he moved lock, stock and barrel to the hills.

Day 367

$\mathcal{A}$ grim-faced Jaidev Roy walked in for a meeting. He took a seat opposite me like a lamb before its slaughter. Gone was the cockiness and cheap arrogance in his demeanour. Soon after the success of Suryankant Joshi's book, Angus had flown in with a mandate for us to expand to twice our size and publish more books. What followed was a mass exodus of editorial and marketing talent from JR Books, as well as from other foreign publishers who lacked a coherent direction on their future. JR Books, in fact, given the debacle of their last 20 new releases and known to have been poor paymasters, was the worst hit, ending up with no one in marketing and editorial. Angus swooped in to buy the rights to the best titles within their existing catalogue and Jaidev Roy was left attempting to reinvent himself as a distributor and a publisher of books translated to regional languages.

'So we've been through your proposal,' I said, 'it makes sense only if we have 10 per cent more of shares, else we could bring on board staff and do it ourselves.'

'No no, of course we can find a middle ground, *haanji*? Can we agree at 7 per cent?'

'I'm afraid not. I've been asked to settle for nothing less than 10 per cent.' *It's a game you've been a pro at, isn't it?*

'*Theek hai*, let's do it. For me the relationship is more important, how does 2-3 per cent matter?' *It's nice to hear this from a miser's mouth.*

'This also includes warehousing and distribution support from your offices in Delhi and Bengaluru, right?' *Squeeze 'em while you can.*

'Yes, of course, just like we discussed earlier. Should I send across the papers for you to sign?' he asked nervously.

'Sure, absolutely! Let's do this,' I said, shaking his hand firmly before I led him out. It was an arrangement that worked for both of us. We did what we were better at, which was finding stories, developing and supporting writing and editorial talent, while he controlled most of the distribution and translation rights, both of which were areas where we had limited expertise.

Zorah called out to me a short while later. We were cutting a cake for Mr Samuel, who had completed 10 years at Kalim and who was now back on the payroll as Production Manager, with two young executives poached from JR Books reporting to him. Sita had moved to a little office of her own, where she focused on managing all contracts and agreements with authors and vendors. We had taken office space across the hall, one that was vacant after the tailor moved to a less expensive workshop.

Zorah and I had talked about taking a bigger apartment, one with a nicer balcony where we could sip chai and water our plants. We also adopted a furry stray pup called Johnny from a kennel run by a bunch of college kids. Thus, the evenings were spent with our new family member, who seemed most satisfied ripping apart my collection of classics and relieving himself on it.

In other updates, we were now an extension of Rahim Khan's family and were often invited for biryani and drinks at their many social dos. Roshan Khan, thrown out of his sprawling penthouse by his ex-wife, continued to sulk and headed off to a rehab clinic in Miami to clean up his act. He returned to begin filming the adaptation of Anya's short story from *Behind Closed Doors*, now shortlisted for The Man Asian Award. Sudhir's book, on the other hand, soon went off the lists and was sold at deep discounts at online stores. The film planned with Roshan Khan was shelved for want of a budget and we politely excused ourselves from publishing the sequel and prequel to his bestseller. Last heard, he was knocking on the doors of Bhojpuri film producers, trying to persuade them to sign a film deal.

Vinod Dutta was conferred the Padma Shri posthumously for his vast contribution to Indian literature and society, which this was accepted by a tearful Ramu, his former caregiver, who also shared a small portion of the mounting royalties from the sale of *Bottled Up*. Anya took a few months off from buying bags and shoes, and showing up at parties, to backpack across Peru with Asmita. Shipra had set up base in Pune to begin efforts on the first school and clinic as part of the Vinod Dutta Trust that received a third of the royalties from their bestseller. Suryakant Joshi, with little to do in the hills, started a blog to share his discourses on the importance of education and contributed generously by way of his royalties to the Vinod Dutta Trust. The authors of *Twilight* lived in hope of being published by us again, while I continued being pursued by bored housewives, grandmothers, retired army colonels, out-of-work crackheads and twits on Twitter who didn't know what spell-check was but all wanting to pen the next bestseller. Naresh Shah was mentioned in a hilarious piece by a magazine that covered the compulsive gatecrasher. He was known to show up at launches and parties uninvited, with a number of business cards that ranged from journalist, inspirational guru, motivation coach and chief marketing officer. Gaurav Bedi's show went off air soon after he suffered a stroke following a heated argument with his hapless cameraman at a literature festival.

Tired from the crazy publishing schedule and appearances from various social dos, Zorah and I left for home early to pack our bags for Shimla. We were due to leave the next morning to spend Christmas at the Governor's House in the hills, where we could also catch up on some skiing. After fussing over little Johnny and handing him over to Rohit and Anita, the new couple in office, we moved to our little balcony to enjoy a cup of chai. I wrapped my arms around Zorah's waist and stared out into the distance, past the crowded streets and the ramshackle buildings, at the lone star that shone in Mumbai's smog-filled skies. I smiled as I remembered the song that had played in the taxi driver's beaten-up Fiat on the day I had arrived in Mumbai:

Jeena yahan, marna yahan
Iske siva, jaana kahan…

My phone rang just then.

'Hello sir, this is Mihin,' a voice said excitedly on the other end. *Who? Oh fuck, it's him!*

'Yes?' *Hang up! Hang up!*

'Happy one-year anniversary at Kalim, sir.'

'Thanks, Mihin!'

'Actually sir, I've written a new book....'

This is home, and there's nowhere else I would rather be.

Acknowledgements

This book has been through a five-year-long journey—from writing the first draft to getting it published. None of this would have been possible without the encouragement of my parents. A note of thanks to my wife, Minaz, and my boys, Zahir and Kabir, who've had to put up with me spending countless hours rewriting or editing the book over the past few months.

Bestseller has been the easiest and most fun book to write and it wouldn't have been possible without the help of the people I've known and met in the publishing industry. I would like to thank Mr Kapish Mehra for believing in this book for five long years, which speaks a lot about his commitment to writers. I would also like to thank Rudra Narayan Sharma, Elina Majumdar and Anurupa Sen from the editorial team at Rupa Publications, who are and always have been a pleasure to work with. I couldn't have brought to life this story without the subtle, but effective and creative, inputs from Meghna Singhee.

A special thanks to Chandan Crasta for his creative, colourful and interesting cover design and his ability to bring the characters in this book to life. A big thanks to those close to me (you know who you are), who've believed in and supported this dream, showered praises, spread the word, been honest with their criticism, pushed me to create and be inspired, even at times when I had put my writing on pause. A heartfelt thanks to those who continue to encourage me—avid readers, book lovers and others who've liked my previous books and reached out to me ever so often.